"I'm Pregnant."

Laying both hands protectively against her flat abdomen, she whispered, "Don't worry about a thing, little guy. You'll be okay. I promise."

Even as she said the words, she felt a flicker of unease as she thought about telling Sam her news. He wouldn't be happy; she knew that already. He was so determined to keep his heart locked away, he would see this baby as an invitation to pain.

Her brain raced with thoughts and wishes and half-baked dreams she knew didn't have a chance at becoming reality. Silently she admitted a secret she'd been hiding not only from Sam but from herself.

She loved Sam Lonergan. She loved everything about him and knew she couldn't keep him.

But at least when he left, she'd have his child.

Dear Reader,

This April, leave the showers behind and embrace the warmth found only in a Silhouette Desire novel. First off is Susan Crosby's *The Forbidden Twin,* the latest installment in the scintillating continuity THE ELLIOTTS. This time, bad girl twin Scarlet sets her heart on seducing the one man she can't have. And speaking of wanting what you can't have, Peggy Moreland's *The Texan's Forbidden Affair* begins a brand-new series for this *USA TODAY* bestselling author. A PIECE OF TEXAS introduces a fabulous Lone Star legacy and stories that will stay with you long after the book is done.

Also launching this month is Maureen Child's SUMMER OF SECRETS, a trilogy about three handsome-as-sin cousins who are in for a season of scandalous revelations...and it all starts with *Expecting Lonergan's Baby.* Katherine Garbera wraps up her WHAT HAPPENS IN VEGAS...series with *Their Million-Dollar Night.* What woman could resist a millionaire who doesn't care about her past as long as she's willing to share his bed?

Making her Silhouette Desire debut this month is Silhouette Intimate Moments and HQN Books author Catherine Mann, with *Baby, I'm Yours.* Her delectable hero is certainly one guy this heroine should think about saying "I do" to once that pregnancy test comes back positive. And rounding out the month with a story of long-denied passion and shocking secrets is Anne Marie Winston's *The Soldier's Seduction.*

Enjoy all we have to offer this month!

Melissa Jeglinski

Melissa Jeglinski
Senior Editor
Silhouette Desire

Please address questions and book requests to:
Silhouette Reader Service
U.S.: 3010 Walden Ave., P.O. Box 1325, Buffalo, NY 14269
Canadian: P.O. Box 609, Fort Erie, Ont. L2A 5X3

MAUREEN CHILD

Expecting
Lonergan's Baby

Published by Silhouette Books

America's Publisher of Contemporary Romance

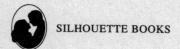

SILHOUETTE BOOKS

ISBN 0-373-76719-6

EXPECTING LONERGAN'S BABY

Visit Silhouette Books at www.eHarlequin.com

Printed in U.S.A.

Books by Maureen Child

MAUREEN CHILD

is a California native who loves to travel. Every chance they get, she and her husband are taking off on another research trip. The author of more than sixty books, Maureen loves a happy ending and still swears that she has the best job in the world. She lives in Southern California with her husband, two children and a golden retriever with delusions of grandeur.

For my family—for always being there.
I love you.

One

Sam Lonergan had expected to find a ghost at the lake. He *hadn't* expected a naked woman.

Given a choice, he much preferred this view. He knew he should look away, but he didn't. Instead he focused his gaze on the long, lean woman slicing through the dark, moonlit water.

Even in the pale wash of moonlight her skin glowed tan and smooth. The water she displaced slipped behind her with hardly a splash. Her arms made long strokes through the water, carrying her from one edge of the small lake and back again to the other. A part of him saw her as a trespasser on holy ground—but another part of him was grateful she was here.

While he watched her, he told himself he shouldn't have come. This lake, this ranch, held too many memories. Too many images that crowded his mind and made remembering an exercise in pain.

Abruptly he squeezed his eyes shut, took a deep breath and slowly released it before opening his eyes again. She'd stopped swimming and was now treading water, watching him watch her.

"Seen enough?" she asked.

"Depends," he told her. "You have anything else to show me?"

Her mouth worked as if she were biting down on words she wouldn't allow herself to say.

"Who are you?" she finally demanded, her voice more angry than worried.

"I could ask you the same thing," he pointed out.

"This is private property."

"Sure is," he agreed, hitching one hip higher than the other and folding his arms over his chest. "So I have to wonder what you're doing on it."

"I live here," she replied, swinging a long, wet fall of dark brown hair back from her face.

Water droplets arced around her head and dropped to the lake like raindrops. It took a minute or two, but her words hit home.

"You live here? This is the Lonergan ranch."

A ranch that had been in his family for generations. Since the early days of the gold rush, when

Sam's great-great-whatever had decided that the real fortune to be found in California was the land—not rocky cold streams where the occasional nugget was discovered.

That Lonergan had settled here, raising horses and a family. A family that now consisted of one old man, one ghost and three Lonergan cousins: Sam, Cooper and Jake.

His grandfather, Jeremiah Lonergan, had lived alone for the last twenty years. Ever since his wife, Sam's grandmother, had died. Now, if a naked woman was to be believed, he had a roommate.

"That's right," she said, warming to her subject. "And the owner of this ranch is *very* protective of me. And *vicious.*"

Sam wanted to laugh. His grandfather was maybe the most gentle-hearted man Sam had ever known. But to hear this woman tell it, Jeremiah was a mad dog.

"Well, he's not here right now, is he?"

"No."

"So since it's just the two of us and we're getting so friendly…mind telling me if you go skinny-dipping often?" he asked instead.

"You spy on naked women often?"

"Whenever I get the chance."

She scowled at him and pushed one hand through her wet hair. She dipped a little lower in the water, and he figured her legs were getting tired of the constant kicking to keep afloat.

"You don't sound ashamed of yourself."

He gave her a lazy smile that didn't go anywhere near his eyes. "Lady, if I *didn't* watch a naked woman when given the opportunity, that'd be something to be ashamed of."

"Your mother must be so proud."

He chuckled. Probably not, but the old man would have been.

She glanced around her and he knew what she was looking at. Emptiness. Except for the oak trees standing like solitary guardians around the ring of the lake, they were alone. The ranch was a good mile east of here, and the highway ten miles south.

"Look," she said and dipped again, the water lapping at the tops of her breasts. "You've had your peep show, but it's cold and I'm tired. I'd like to get out now."

"Who's stopping you?"

Her eyes went wide and dark. "Hello? I'm not getting out of this water with you watching me."

Something like guilt nibbled at the edges of a conscience that was already too noisy. But he ignored it. Yes, he should look away, but would a starving man turn down a steak just because it was stolen?

"You could turn your back," she said a moment later.

One corner of his mouth lifted. "Now, if I do that,

how do I know you won't hit me over the head with something?"

"Does it *look* like I'm carrying a concealed weapon?"

He shrugged. "A man can't be too careful."

She nodded, dipped low enough to have the surface of the water lap at her throat, then muttered, "Perfect. I'm naked and *you're* the one threatened."

A wind kicked up out of nowhere, rustling the leaves on the oaks until it sounded as if they were surrounded by a whispering crowd. She shivered and dipped even lower in the water, and another ping of guilt echoed inside Sam.

He tipped his head back to look at the star-studded sky before looking at her again. "It's a nice night. Maybe I'll camp out right here."

"You wouldn't."

"No?" Beginning to enjoy himself, he pretended to consider it. "Maybe not. But the question remains. You getting out of the lake or do you know how to sleep while treading water?"

She huffed out a disgusted breath and slapped one hand against the water. "I'm getting out."

"Can't wait."

"You're a real jerk, you know that?"

"That's been said before."

"Color me surprised."

"You're still in the water." He unfolded his arms

and stuck both hands into the back pockets of his jeans. "Must be getting pretty cold about now."

"Yeah, but—"

"Told you I'm not going anywhere."

She gave another quick glance around at the dark country surrounding them, as if hoping to catch a glimpse of the cavalry riding to her rescue.

"How do I know you won't attack me the minute I get out of the lake?" she asked, eyes narrowed on him.

"I could give you my word," Sam said, "but since you don't know me, that wouldn't be worth much."

She studied him for a long minute and he had the weird sensation that she was looking far more deeply than he would like. But after another long minute she said, "If you give me your word, I'll believe you."

Frowning, he pulled one hand from his pocket and scrubbed the back of his neck. A beautiful, naked trespasser trusted him. Great. "Fine. You have it."

She nodded, but another long minute or two ticked past before she started in toward shore. Something inside him quickened. Anticipation? Excitement? It had been long enough since he'd felt either, he couldn't be sure. But the moment came and went so fast, he couldn't explore it or even take a second to enjoy it.

Moonlight dazzled on her wet golden skin as she walked out of the water and up the short incline to where her clothes were stacked in a neat little pile.

He watched her and felt a hot, pulsing need rush through him with enough force to stagger him.

She was tall and lean, with small, firm breasts, narrow hips and a tan line that told him she didn't usually skinny-dip. He could only be grateful that she'd chosen to tonight. Somehow those tan lines made her nudity that much more exciting. Paler strips of skin against the honey-brown tempted a man to define the edges of those lines.

Desire stirred and heat pooled inside him.

She was magical in the moonlight, and it took everything he had to keep from grabbing her up and pulling her close. It was like watching a mermaid step out of the sea just long enough to tempt a man.

"You are amazing."

She faltered slightly, then lifted her chin and stood tall and proud, no embarrassment, no hesitation. And Sam knew he should feel guilty for staring at her, taking advantage of the situation.

But damned if he could.

In seconds, she'd yanked on a T-shirt and stepped into a soft-looking cotton skirt that swirled around her knees as she bent to pull on first one sandal and then the other.

Hell, he should be thanking her. She'd taken his mind off the past, made facing this lake and the memories again much easier than he'd expected.

"Look," he said as she straightened up, "I'm sorry

for giving you a hard time, but seeing you here surprised me and—"

She slugged him in the stomach.

Didn't hurt much, but since he was unprepared, all his air left him in a rush.

"*I* surprised *you?*" Maggie Collins grabbed her long brown hair, held the mass off to one side and quickly wrung the excess water from it before flipping it all over her shoulder again.

Amazing. He'd called her *amazing*.

She could still feel the flush of something warm and delicious as he watched her. It was as if she'd felt his touch, not just his gaze, locked on her. And for just one brief moment she'd *wanted* him to touch her. To feel his hands sliding over her wet skin.

Which only made her madder. She looked him up and down dismissively, then lifted her chin. "You rotten, self-serving, miserable…" Oh, she hated when she ran out of invectives before she was finished.

Inhaling sharply, she threw her shoulders back and gathered up her tattered pride. She'd about had a heart attack when she'd first seen him, standing on shore, watching her in the darkness. But the initial jolt of fear had subsided quickly enough the longer she'd looked at him.

Maggie'd been on her own long enough to develop a sort of radar that told her when she was safe and when she was in danger. And none of her internal warning bells had gone off, despite the fact that he hadn't been gentleman enough to either leave or turn around.

He wasn't dangerous.

At least not physically.

Emotionally—now that might be a different story. He was tall and gorgeous—already worrisome—and then there was the gleam in his dark eyes. Not just the flash of desire she'd seen and noted—but an undercurrent of something sad and empty. Maggie'd always been attracted to wounded guys. The ones with sad eyes and lonely hearts.

But after getting her own heart bruised a few times, she'd decided that sometimes there was a *reason* men were alone. Now all she had to do was remember that.

She stood her ground, glaring at the man who'd intruded on her nightly swim. Just a few years ago she might have skittered away quickly, trying to disappear. But not now. In the last two years things had changed for her. She'd found a home. She *belonged* on the Lonergan ranch, and no one—let alone a surly, good-looking stranger—would scare her off.

"You've got a good right jab," he conceded.

"You'll live." She started past him, headed for the line of trees and the path beyond that would lead her back to the ranch house.

He stopped her with a hand on her arm. Instantly

her skin sizzled and her blood bubbled in her veins. She yanked free of his grasp and took a step back just for good measure.

"Hey, hey," he said, his voice soothing as he lifted both hands in mock surrender. "It's okay. Relax."

The quick jolt of adrenaline she'd felt at his unexpected touch was already dissipating when she glared at him. "Just...don't grab me."

"No problem." he said, "Won't happen again."

She blew out a breath and willed herself to calm down. It wasn't just the fact that he'd surprised her by taking hold of her arm—it was the sudden flash of heat that had dazzled up her arm only to ricochet throughout her body. She'd never felt that punch of awareness before and wasn't sure she liked it much. Better to just get away from the man. Fast.

"It's going to take me about ten minutes to walk back to the house," she said when she was certain her voice wouldn't quiver. "I suggest you use that time to get gone."

He shook his head. "Can't do it."

"You'd better. Because the minute I get to a phone, I'll be calling the police to report a trespasser."

"You could," he said and fell into step beside her as she once again started for the tree line. "But it wouldn't do any good."

"And why's that?"

"Because," he said, coming to a stop, "I went to

high school with half the police force in town. And I think Jeremiah Lonergan might just object to you having me arrested."

A sinking sensation opened in the pit of her stomach, but Maggie asked the question anyway. "Why would he object?"

"Because I'm Sam Lonergan, and Jeremiah's my grandfather."

Two

Everything else faded away but a rush of anger that nearly strangled Maggie. She'd known, of course, that all three of Jeremiah's grandsons were arriving this summer, but she hadn't expected one of them to sneak in under the cover of darkness and then turn out to be a Peeping Tom.

"If I'd known who you were," Maggie snapped, "I would have hit you harder."

"Lucky for me I kept quiet then."

"How could you do this to him?" she demanded, planting both hands on her hips.

"Do what?"

"Stay away," she snapped. "You—*all* of you. Not

one of the three of you has so much as visited your grandfather in two years."

"And you know this how?"

"Because I've been here," she said, slapping one hand to her chest. "Me. I've been taking care of that sweet old man for two years and I don't remember tripping over any of you in the house."

"Sweet old man?" His laughter shot from his throat. "Jeremiah Lonergan is the most softhearted, crustiest old goat in the country."

"He is *not*," she shouted, infuriated by his amusement at the expense of an old man who had been even lonelier than she had when she first met him. "He's sweet. And kind. And caring. And *alone*. His own family doesn't care enough to come and see him. You should all be ashamed of yourselves. Especially *you*. You're a *doctor*. You should have come home before this to make sure he was all right. But no. You wait until he's…" God. She couldn't even bring herself to say the word *dying*.

She couldn't think about losing Jeremiah. Couldn't bear the thought of losing him and the home she'd come to love so much. And here stood a man who took all of that for granted. Who didn't appreciate the love that was waiting for him. Who didn't care enough about that sweet old man to even *visit*.

New fury pumped through her and she narrowed

her eyes on the man who only moments before had stirred her blood into a simmering boil.

His laughter faded away and a scowl that was both fierce and irritated twisted his features. "Just who the hell are you anyway?"

"My name's Maggie Collins," she said, straightening up to her full five feet four inches. "And I'm your grandfather's housekeeper."

And she had that position because the "crusty old goat" had taken a chance on her when she'd needed it most. So she wasn't about to stand by and let *anyone,* even his grandson, berate the old man she loved.

"Well, Maggie Collins," he said through gritted teeth, "just because you've been taking care of Jeremiah's house doesn't mean you know squat about me or my family."

She leaned in at him, not intimidated in the slightest. In the last two years she'd watched Jeremiah flip through old photo albums, stare at home movies, lose himself in the past because the grandsons he loved didn't care enough to give him a present.

And it infuriated her that three grown men who had the home she'd always longed for didn't seem to appreciate it.

"I know that though the man has three grandsons, he's *alone.* I know that he had to take in a *stranger* to keep him company. I know that he looks at pictures of the three of you and his heart aches."

She poked him in the chest with her index finger. "I know that it took his being near death's door—" her breath hitched and she hiccupped "—to get you all back here to see him this summer. I know *that* much."

Sam shoved one hand through his long dark hair, looked away from her for a slow count of ten. Then, when he turned his gaze back to her, the anger had left him. His eyes were dark and shadowed.

"You're right."

She hadn't expected that and it took her aback a little. Tipping her head to one side, she studied him. "Just like that? I'm right?"

"To a point," he admitted and his voice dropped, wrapping the two of them in a kind of insular seclusion. "It's…*complicated,*" he said finally.

So much for being surprised into feeling just a tiny bit of sympathy for his side of the story. Disgusted, she shook her head. "No, it's not. He's your grandfather. He loves you. And you ignore him."

"You don't understand."

"You're absolutely right." She folded her arms across her chest, tapped her foot against the rocky ground and waited.

His eyes narrowed. "I don't owe you an explanation, Maggie Collins, so don't bother waiting for one."

No, he didn't, though she desperately wanted one. She couldn't understand how anyone with a home, a

family, could deliberately avoid them. "Fine. Maybe
you don't owe me anything, but you certainly owe
your grandfather."

That scowl deepened until it looked as though it
had been carved into his face. "I'm here, aren't I?"

"Finally. Have you seen him yet?"

"No," he admitted, shoving both hands into his
pockets as he shifted his gaze to the lake behind
them. "I haven't. I had to come here first. Had to face
this place first."

And just like that, Maggie's heart twisted. She knew
what he was seeing when he looked at the small lake.
She knew what he was remembering because Jeremiah
had told her everything there was to know about his
grandsons. The good, the bad and the haunting.

"I'm sorry," she blurted, wishing she could pull at
least *some* of her harsher words back. "I know how
hard this must be for you, but—"

He cut her off with a look. "You don't know," he
said tightly. "You *can't*. So why don't you go back
to the house. Tell my grandfather I'll be there soon."

He walked away to stand at the water's edge,
staring out over the black, still surface of the lake. His
pain reached out to her and she flinched from it. She
didn't want to feel sorry for him. Didn't want to give
him the benefit of the doubt. Though even if he did
have his reasons for avoiding the Lonergan ranch, she

thought, that didn't make it all right for him to avoid the old man who loved him.

Her sympathy evaporated and Maggie left him there, alone in the shadows.

Jeremiah just had time to shove the blood-curdling horror novel he'd been reading under his covers before Maggie opened his bedroom door after a brief knock. He watched the girl he'd come to think of as a granddaughter and smiled to himself. Her dark brown hair was wet, trailing dampness across her T-shirt. Her long, flowing skirt was wrinkled and dotted with dried bits of grass, and her sandals squeaked with the water seeping into the leather.

"Been down to the lake again, eh?" he asked as she came closer and straightened the quilt and sheet covering him.

She smiled but couldn't quite hide the flash of something else in her dark eyes.

"What is it, Maggie?" He grabbed her hand, making sure to be as feeble as possible, as she reached for the glass pitcher on his bedside table. "Are you all right?"

"I'm fine," she said, pulling her hand free and giving him a pat before carrying the carafe to the adjoining bathroom to fill it with fresh water. She stepped back into the bedroom and walked quickly back to his side. "I met your grandson, that's all."

Jeremiah's heart lifted, but he remembered just in

time that he was supposed to be a dying man now. Keeping his voice quiet, he asked, "Which one?"

"Sam."

"Ah." He smiled to himself. "Well, where is he? Didn't he come back with you?"

"No," she said, frowning as she turned the bedside lamp with the three-way bulb down to its lowest setting. Instantly the room fell into shadows, the pale night light hardly reaching her, standing right at his bedside. "He said he wanted to stay at the lake for a while first."

Jeremiah felt a twinge of pain in his heart and knew that it was only a shadow of the pain Sam must be feeling at the moment. But damn it, fifteen years had gone by. It was time the Lonergan cousins put the past to rest. Long past time, if truth be told. And if he'd had to lie to get them all to come here, well, then, it was a lie told with the best of reasons.

"How'd he look?"

Maggie fidgeted quickly with his pillows, then straightened up, put her hands on her narrow hips and said thoughtfully, "Alone. Like the most *alone* man I've ever seen."

"Suppose he is." Sighing, Jeremiah let his head fall back against the pillows that Maggie had plumped so neatly. He should feel guilty about tricking all of his grandsons into coming home. But he didn't. Hell, if you couldn't be sneaky when you got old, what the hell good were you?

"It's not going to be easy," he said. "Not on any of 'em. But they're strong men. They'll make it through."

Maggie gave the quilt covering him one last tug, then leaned down and planted a quick kiss on his forehead. "They're not the ones I'm worried about," she said, then stood up and smiled down at him.

"You're a good girl, Maggie. But you don't need to worry about me. I'll be fine once my boys are home."

Sam entered the house quietly, half expecting the old man's bodyguard to leap at him from the shadows, teeth bared. When there was no sign of Maggie Collins, though, he surrendered to the inevitable and glanced around the room he'd once run wild through.

Two lamps had been left burning, their soft glow illuminating a room he would have been able to find his way through blindfolded. Nothing had changed. Oak floors, scarred from years of running children and booted feet, were dotted with faded colorful throw rugs. Four dark brown leather sofas sat arranged in a huge square, with a table wide enough to be a raft in the dead center of them. Magazines were stacked neatly in one corner of the table and a vase of yellow roses sat center stage.

Had to be the bodyguard's doing, he told himself, since he knew damn well Jeremiah wouldn't have thought to cut fresh flowers. Maggie Collins's face rose up in his mind, then faded away as Sam looked around the house, familiarizing himself all over again with his past.

A river-stone hearth wide and high enough for a man to stand in dominated one wall, and a few embers still glowed richly red behind a fire screen of scrolled iron. The walls were adorned with framed family photos and landscapes painted by a talented, if young, hand. Sam winced at the paintings and quickly looked away. He wasn't ready just yet to be smothered by ghosts. It was enough that he was here. He'd have to swallow the past in small gulps or he'd choke on them.

Dropping his duffle bag by the door, he headed for the stairs at the far end of the room. Each stair was a log, sawn in half and varnished to a high sheen. The banisters looked like petrified tree trunks, and his hand slid along the cool surface as he mounted the stairs to the bedrooms above.

His steps sounded like the slow beating of his own heart. Every move he made took him closer to memories he didn't want to look at. Yet there was no going back. No avoiding it anymore.

At the head of the stairs he paused and glanced down the long hall. Closed doors were all that greeted him, but he knew the rooms behind those doors as well as he knew his own reflection in the mirror. He and his cousins had shared those rooms every summer for most of their lives. They'd crashed up the stairs, slid down the banisters and run wild across every acre of the family ranch.

Until that last summer.

The day when everything had changed forever.

The day they'd all grown up—and apart.

Scowling, he brushed away the memories as he would a cloud of gnats in front of his face and walked to the door at the head of the stairs. His grandfather's room. A man he hadn't seen in fifteen years.

Shame rippled through him and he told himself that Maggie Collins would be proud if she knew it. She was right about one thing. They shouldn't have stayed away from the old man for so long. Should have found a way to see him despite the pain.

But they hadn't.

Instead they'd punished themselves, and in the doing had punished an old man who hadn't deserved it, as well.

He knocked and waited.

"Sam?"

The voice was weaker than he'd thought it would be but still so familiar. Apparently the house-keeper/bodyguard had spilled the news about his arrival. He opened the door, stepped inside and felt his heart turn over in his chest.

Jeremiah Lonergan. The strongest man Sam had ever known looked...*old*. Most of his hair was gone, his tanned scalp shining in the soft lamplight. A fringe of gray hair ringed his head, and the lines that had always defined his face were deeper, scored more fully into his features. He looked small in the wide bed, covered in one of the quilts his wife had made decades ago.

Sam felt the solid punch of sorrow slam him in the gut. Time had passed. Too much time. And for that one startling moment he deeply regretted all the years he'd missed with the man he'd always loved. For some reason, he hadn't really expected that Jeremiah would be different. Despite the phone call from the old man's doctor saying that he didn't have much time left, Sam had thought somehow that his grandfather would be unchanged.

"Hi, Pop," he said and forced a smile.

"Come in, come in," his grandfather urged, weakly waving one hand. Then he patted the edge of the bed. "Sit down, boy. Let me look at you."

Sam did and, once he was close enough, gave his grandfather a quick once-over. He was thinner, but his eyes were clear and sharp. His tan wasn't as dark as it had been, but there was no sickly pallor to his cheeks. His hands were gnarled, but they weren't trembling.

All good things.

"How you feeling?" Sam asked, reaching out to lay one hand on his grandfather's forehead.

Jeremiah brushed that hand away. "Fine. I'm fine. And I've already got me a doctor to poke and prod. Don't need my grandson doing it, too."

"Sorry," Sam said with a shrug. "Professional hazard." As a doctor, he could respect another doctor's territory and not want to intrude. As a grandson, he wanted to see for himself that his grandfather was all right. Apparently, though, that wouldn't be as easy as it sounded. "I spoke to Dr. Evans after I talked to you last month. He says that your heart's in pretty bad shape."

Jeremiah winced. "Doctors. Don't pay them any mind."

Sam laughed shortly. "Thanks."

"Don't mean you, boy," the old man corrected quickly. "I'm sure you're a fine doctor. Always been real proud of you, Sam. In fact, I was telling Bert Evans that you might be just the man to buy him out."

Sam stood up and shoved both hands in his pockets. He'd been afraid of this. Afraid that the old man would make more of this visit than there was. Afraid he'd ask Sam to stay. Expect him to stay. And Sam couldn't. Wouldn't.

But his grandfather either didn't notice his discomfort or didn't care. Because he kept talking. And with every word, guilt pinged around inside Sam just a little bit harder.

"Bert's a good doc, mind. But he's as old as me and getting ready to fold up shop." He smiled up at Sam and winked conspiratorially. "The town needs a doctor, and seeing as you don't have a place of your own—"

"Pop, I'm not staying." Sam forced himself to say it flat out. He didn't want to hurt his grandfather, but he didn't want the old man holding onto false hopes either. Guilt tore at him to see the gleam go out of his grandfather's eyes. "I'm here for the summer," he said softly, willing the old man to understand just what it had cost him to come home again. "But when it's over, I'm leaving again."

"I thought…" Jeremiah's voice trailed away as he sagged back into his pillows. "I thought that once I got you back here, you'd see it's where you belong. Where all of you belong."

Pain rippled through Sam in tiny waves, one after the other. There was a time once, when he was a kid, that he would have done anything to live here forever. To be a part of the little town that had once seemed so perfect to him. To know that this house would always be his.

But those dreams died one bright summer day fifteen years ago.

Now he didn't belong anywhere.

"I'm sorry, Pop," he said, knowing it wasn't enough but that it was all he had to offer.

The old man looked at him for a long time before finally closing his eyes on a tired sigh. "It's a long summer, boy. Anything might happen."

"Don't make plans for me, Jeremiah," Sam warned, though it cost him to hurt the man again. "I won't stay. I can't. And you know why."

"I know why you think that," he said, his voice a weary sigh. "And I know you're wrong. All of you are. But a man's got to find his own way." He slipped down farther beneath the quilt. "I'm feeling tired now, so why don't you come see me tomorrow and we'll talk some more."

"Jeremiah…"

"Go on now," he whispered. "Go down and get yourself something to eat. I'll still be here in the morning."

When his grandfather closed his eyes, effectively ending any more tries at talking, Sam had no choice. He turned and headed for the door, let himself out and quietly closed the door behind him. He'd been in the house less than fifteen minutes and already he'd upset an old man with a bad heart.

Good job.

But he couldn't let his grandfather count on him staying. Couldn't give Jeremiah the promise of a future when the past was so thick around Sam he could hardly see the present.

He'd long since become accustomed to living with memories that haunted him. But he'd never be able to live here again—where he'd see a ghost around every corner.

Three

Maggie sat in her living room and stared across the yard at the main ranch house. No more than twenty feet of ground separated the two buildings, but at the moment it felt like twenty *miles*.

In the two years she'd lived at the Lonergan ranch she'd never felt more of an outsider. Never felt as *alone* as she had that first day when her car had finally gasped its last and died right outside the main gate.

Tears were close. Maggie was out of money and now out of transportation. Though she had nowhere in particular to go, up until five minutes ago she'd have been able to get there.

Staring up and down the long, empty road,

edged on both sides by open fields, she fought a rising tide of despair that threatened to choke her. The afternoon sun was hot and reflected back off the narrow highway until she felt as though she were standing in an oven. No trees shaded the road, and the last sign she'd passed had promised that the town of Coleville was still twenty-five miles away.

Just thinking about the long walk ahead of her made her tired. But sitting down and having a good long cry wouldn't get her any closer to town. And feeling sorry for herself would only get her a stuffed-up nose and red eyes. Nope. Maggie Collins didn't waste time on self-pity. Instead she kept trying. Kept searching. Knowing that someday, somewhere, she'd find the place where she belonged. Where she could plant herself and grow some roots. The kind of roots she'd always wanted as a child.

But to earn those roots she had to get off her duff. Resigned, she opened up the car door and grabbed her navy-blue backpack off the floor of the passenger seat.

"Looks like that car's about had it."

She hit her head on the roof of the old car as she backed out and straightened up all in one motion. The old man who'd spoken stood just a few feet from her, leaning against one of the whitewashed posts holding up a sign that proclaimed Lonergan. She hadn't even heard him approach, which told her that either he was more spry than he looked or she was even more tired than she felt.

Probably the latter.

He wasn't very tall. He wore a battered hat that shaded his lined, leathery face and his watchful dark eyes. His blue jeans were faded and worn, and his boots looked as if they were older than him.

"It just die on you?" he asked with a wave of one tanned hand at the car.

"Yeah," she said after seeing the quiet glint of kindness in his dark brown eyes. "Not surprising, really. It's been on borrowed time for the last few hundred miles."

He looked her up and down—not in a threatening way, she thought later, but as a man might look at a lost child while he thought about how to help her.

Finally he said, "Can't do anything about that car of yours, but if you'd care to come up to the house, maybe we can rustle up some lunch."

She glanced back down the road at the emptiness stretching out in either direction, then back at the man waiting quietly for her to make up her mind. Maggie'd learned at an early age to trust her instincts, and every one she had was telling her to take a chance. What did she have to lose? Besides, if he turned out to be a weirdo, she was pretty sure she could outrun him.

"I can't pay you for the food," she said, lifting her

*chin and meeting his gaze with the only thing she had
left—her pride. "But I'd be happy to do some chores
for you in exchange."*

*One corner of his mouth lifted and his face fell
into familiar laugh lines that crinkled at the edges of
his eyes. "I think we can work something out."*

Maggie sighed at the memory and leaned her head
back against the overstuffed cushion of the big chair.
Curling her legs up beneath her, she looked around
the small cottage that had been her sanctuary for the
last two years. A guesthouse, Jeremiah had offered
it to her that first day. By the end of the lunch she'd
prepared for them, he'd given her a job and this little
house to call her own. And for two years they'd done
well together.

She turned her head and for the first time saw a
light other than the one in Jeremiah's bedroom
burning in the darkness. And she wondered what
Sam Lonergan's arrival was going to do to her world.

The scent of coffee woke him up.

Sam rolled over in the big bed and stared blankly
at the ceiling. For a minute or two he couldn't place
where he was. Nothing new for him, though. A man
who traveled as much as he did got used to waking
up in strange places.

Then familiarity sneaked in and twisted at his
heart, his guts. The room hadn't changed much from

when he was a kid. Whitewashed oak-plank walls, dotted with posters of sports heroes and one impossibly endowed swimsuit beauty, surrounded him. A desk on the far wall still held a plastic model of the inner workings of the human body, and the twin bookcases were stuffed with paperback mysteries and thrillers sharing space alongside medical dictionaries and old textbooks.

He threw one arm across his eyes and winced at the sharp jab of pain as memories prodded and poked inside him. A part of him was listening, half expecting to hear long-silent voices. His cousins, shouting to him from their rooms along the hall. It had always been like that during the summers they spent together.

The four Lonergan boys—as close as brothers. Born during a three-year clump, they'd grown up seeing each other every summer on the Lonergan ranch. Their fathers were brothers, and though none of them felt the pull for the ranch where they'd grown up, their sons had.

This was a world apart from everyday life. Where the land rolled open for miles, inviting boys to hop on their bikes to explore. There were small-town fairs, and fireworks and baseball games. There was working in the fields, helping with the horses Jeremiah had once kept and swimming in the lake.

At that thought, everything in Sam seized up. His heart went cold and air struggled to enter his lungs. It was harder than he thought it would be, being here. Seeing everything the same and yet so different.

"Shouldn't have come," he muttered, his voice sounding scratchy and raw to his own ears. But then, how could he *not?* The old man was in bad shape and he needed his grandsons. There was simply no way to deny him that.

Fifteen years he'd been gone and this room looked as though he'd left it fifteen *minutes* ago. It's a hard thing for a grown man to come into the room he'd left as a boy. Especially when he'd left that room under a black cloud of guilt and pain.

But none of this was making it any easier on him.

"Not supposed to be easy," he muttered, tossing the quilt covering him aside so he could stand up and face the first day of what promised to be the longest summer of his life.

From downstairs came the homey sounds of pans rattling and soft footsteps against the hardwood floor. The aroma of coffee seemed thicker now, heavier, though it was probably only that he was awake enough now to really hunger for it.

Had to be the water nymph in the kitchen.

Jeremiah's housekeeper.

The woman he'd seen naked.

The woman he'd dreamed about all night.

Hell. He ought to thank her for that alone. With her

in his mind, his brain had for once been too busy to torture him with images of another face. Another time.

Grabbing up his jeans, he yanked them on, then pulled on a white T-shirt and shoved his arms through the sleeves. Not bothering with shoes, he headed down the hall, pausing briefly at his grandfather's closed bedroom door before continuing on toward the kitchen.

He needed coffee.

And maybe he needed something else, too. Another look at the mermaid?

His bare feet didn't make a sound on the stairs, so he approached her quietly enough that she didn't know he was watching her. Morning sunlight spilled through the shining windowpanes and lay like a golden blanket across the huge round pedestal table and the warm wood floor. Everything in the room practically glistened, and he had to admit that as a housekeeper, she seemed to be doing a hell of a job. The counters were tidy, the floor polished till it shone and even the ancient appliances looked almost new. The walls had been painted a bright, cheery yellow, and the stiffly starched white curtains at the windows nearly crackled in the breeze drifting under the partially opened sash.

But it was the woman who had Sam's attention. Just as she had the night before. She moved around the old kitchen with a familiarity that at once pleased and irritated him.

Not exactly rational, but it was early. A part of Sam was glad his grandfather had had this woman here, looking out for him. And another completely illogical side of him resented that she was so much at home on the Lonergan ranch when he felt...on edge.

Her long dark hair was gathered into a neat braid that fell down the center of her back, ending at her shoulder blades. A bright red ribbon held the end of the braid together and made a colorful splash against the pale blue shirt she wore tucked into a pair of the most worn, faded jeans he'd ever seen. Threadbare in patches, the jeans hugged her behind and clung to her long legs like a desperate lover.

An old Stones tune poured quietly from the radio on the counter, and as Sam watched, the mermaid did a quick little dance and swiveled her hips in time to the music. His breath caught as his gaze locked on her behind and he found himself praying that one of those threadbare patches would give way, giving him another glimpse of her tanned skin.

Then she did a slow spin, caught a glimpse of him. And the smile on her face faded.

"Do you always sneak up on people or am I just special?"

Sam scrubbed one hand over his face, as if that would be enough to get his brain away from the tantalizing thoughts it had been entertaining.

"Didn't want to interrupt the floor show," he said

tightly, hoping she wouldn't hear the edge of hunger in his voice. He walked past her and headed straight for the coffeepot on the counter.

As the Stones song drifted into an R&B classic, he filled a heavy white mug with the coffee, took a sip, then turned around to face her. Leaning back against the counter, he crossed one bare foot over the other and asked, "You always dance in the kitchen?"

She huffed in a breath and tightened her grip on the spatula she held in her right hand. "When I'm *alone.*"

"Like the skinny-dipping, huh?"

Glaring at him, she said, "A gentleman wouldn't remind me of that."

"And a gentleman wouldn't have looked," he reminded her as the image of her wet, pale, honeyed skin rose up in his mind. "I did. Remember?"

"I'm not likely to forget."

One eyebrow lifted as he swept his gaze up and down her quickly, thoroughly. "Me, neither."

She opened her mouth to speak, then shut it again and took a deep breath. He could almost see her counting to ten to get a grip on the temper flashing in her eyes. Eyes, he noticed, that in the morning light weren't as dark as he'd thought the night before. They were brown but not. More the color of good single-malt scotch.

He took another gulp of coffee and told himself to get a grip.

"You're deliberately trying to pick a fight," she said. "Why?"

He frowned into his coffee. "Because I'm not a nice man."

"That's not what your grandfather says."

He looked at her. "Jeremiah's prejudiced. And a hell of a storyteller. Don't believe half of what he tells you."

"He told me you're a doctor. Is that right?"

"Yeah." Frowning still, he took another sip of really superior coffee. "I am."

"Did you—" she paused and waited for him to look at her "—examine him last night?"

He laughed, and that short burst of sound surprised him as much as it did her. "Me? Not a chance. Jeremiah still thinks of me as the thirteen-year-old kid who slapped a homemade plaster cast on his golden retriever."

"You didn't."

He smiled to himself, remembering. "I really did. Made it out of papier-mâché. Just practicing," he said, remembering how Jeremiah's golden, Storm, had sat patiently, letting Sam do his worst. "Pop took it off before it had a chance to dry."

She was smiling at him and her eyes looked… shiny. Something in him shifted, gave way, and uncomfortable, Sam straightened up and gulped at his coffee again. "Anyway, the point is, Jeremiah won't let me touch him. I'll talk to his doctor, though. Get what information I can."

"Good." She nodded and turned to stir the eggs, a golden foamy layer in the skillet on the stove. "I mean, it's good that you can check. I'm worried. He's been so…"

"What?"

She turned around to look at him again. "It's not something I can put my finger on and say, *There. That's different. That's wrong.* It's just that he's not the same lately. He seems a little more tired. A little more…fragile somehow."

"He's closing in on seventy," Sam reminded her and scowled to himself as he realized just how much time had slipped past him.

"And up until two weeks ago," she said, "you wouldn't have known it. Up at sunrise, doing chores, driving into town to have lunch with Dr. Evans, square dancing on Friday night."

"Square dancing?" Another surprise and another flicker of irritation that this woman knew so much more about his grandfather than *he* did.

She waved one hand at him while she stirred the eggs. "He and some of his friends go to the senior center in Fresno on Fridays." She paused and sighed. "At least, he *used* to."

"Maybe it's nothing," he said, and wasn't sure which of them he was trying to console.

"I hope so."

He heard the hope in her voice and was touched that she cared so deeply. "You really love him, don't you?"

"I really do." She turned her back on the stove and faced him. "Look, *Sam.*" She said his name firmly, as if forcing herself to make a connection that she really wasn't interested in. "You're here to see your grandfather and I'm glad. For *his* sake."

He shifted, pushing away from the counter to stand on his own two feet. "But…?"

"*But…*" she said, turning for the stove and the pan that was beginning to smoke, "I think that we should try to stay out of each other's way while you're here."

"Is that right?" He stepped up alongside her and he *felt* tension ripple between them. Damn it. He didn't need this. Didn't want it. And he'd had every intention of steering clear of the little housekeeper. Until she'd suggested it.

Maggie stirred the scrambled eggs quickly, flipping them over and over again in the cast-iron skillet until they were a golden-brown and dry, just the way Jeremiah liked them. She tried to keep her mind on her cooking, but with Sam standing so close, it wasn't easy.

She'd made up her mind last night that the one sure way to protect her place on this ranch was to stay out of the way this summer. She didn't want to give any of the Lonergan cousins reason to think that their grandfather would be better off with someone other than her taking care of him.

She'd lain awake in her bed most of the night, thinking about this place and what it meant to her. About the old man who had become her family.

And if she were to be completely honest, sometime around dawn she'd thought about Sam. About the way she'd felt when he'd looked at her walking naked from the water.

About the swirl of heat that had swept through her, making the chill wind nothing more than a whisper. And she'd wondered what it would feel like to have him touch her, smooth his hands over her skin, dip his fingers into her—

"The eggs are burning."

"What?" She blinked, stared at the pan and instinctively used her free hand to push it off the flame.

Instantly pain bristled on her palm and she dropped the spatula to cradle her left hand against her chest. Tears clouded her eyes and a whimper squeaked past her lips.

"Damn it!" Sam set his coffee cup on the stove, grabbed her left hand, looked at it, then dragged her with him across the kitchen to the sink. He turned on the cold water and held her hand beneath the icy stream. Instantly the pain subsided and she sighed.

"What the hell were you thinking?"

"I don't know," she said, wiggling her fingers in an effort to pull her hand free of his tight grasp. It didn't work. "I just—"

"Doesn't look bad," he said, smoothing his fingers over the palm of her hand with a tenderness that touched something deep inside her. "Hold still and let me be sure."

The doctor in him took over, she noticed, as the cranky man became suddenly all business.

Then something shifted. Something changed.

His touch became less professional and more... personal. He turned her hand beneath the flow of water, inspecting every inch of her skin. And Maggie closed her eyes against the twin sensations rushing through her. The cold of the water numbed her even as the heat of Sam's touch engulfed her. Her breath staggered a little as she felt his fingertips glide across her wet skin with a gentleness that she'd never known before.

She opened her eyes to find him staring at her. Their gazes locked and a thread of something warm and unspoken drew tight between them. Her breath staggered out of her lungs and her heartbeat thundered in her ears. After what felt like a small eternity, she couldn't bear the tension-filled silence anymore. Mouth dry, voice croaking, she asked, "Is my hand okay?"

"You were lucky." His voice was a low growl of sound that seemed to reverberate around the room. "There's no blistering."

"Good," she managed to say while she locked her knees so they wouldn't wobble and give out on her. God. Was the air really hot? Or was it just her own blood boiling? Oh, yeah, going to keep her distance this summer. Nice start to that plan.

His fingers continued to stroke and soothe her skin and she felt that touch all the way to the center of her. Strange. She'd never experienced anything like this before. A simple touch shouldn't turn her insides to mush.

At last, he turned off the water and reached for a dish towel. Holding her hand in his, he used the soft linen to blot her skin dry. Then he lifted his gaze to hers again, and Maggie felt a jolt of something amazing pass between them just before he dropped her hand as if it was a rattler and took a step back.

"You'll be fine," he said, pushing one hand through his hair. "Just be more careful, okay?"

"I usually am."

"Right." He paused, took a breath and said, "Look, about last night—"

Her head snapped up and her gaze locked with his. "What?"

He studied her for a long minute before lowering his gaze. "Nothing. Never mind. Probably better all around if we just forgot last night ever happened."

Sure. Pretend he hadn't seen her naked. No problem. "Probably would."

"Yeah." He tossed the towel to the counter, then shoved both hands into the back pockets of his jeans, as if unwilling to risk touching her again. "I'm thinking you're right about something, too. Better if we just stayed out of each other's way this summer."

"Okay." Maggie was still struggling to even out her breath and convince her heart to slide down back into her chest where it belonged. Apparently, though, Sam Lonergan had much quicker recuperative powers. Because he could pretend all he wanted— she *knew* he'd felt something as powerful as she had.

"Fine. Then we're agreed." He glanced around the room as if he didn't remember where he was. Then, shaking his head, he crossed the room and grabbed up his coffee cup. Stalking to the counter, he refilled it, then passed her on his way out of the room. He stopped in the doorway and looked back at her. "I'm going to grab a quick shower. Then I'm headed into Coleville. Want to talk to Jeremiah's doctor."

She nodded, but he was already leaving the room with steps so quick his feet might have been on fire. Apparently she wasn't the only one a little flustered by what had just happened.

She'd thought that Sam Lonergan could be a threat to the home she loved so much.

But she hadn't expected him to be an entirely different kind of threat to her sanity.

Four

He took an ice-cold shower.

It didn't help.

Damn it, things were going to be hard enough this summer without worrying about the sexy little housekeeper with whiskey-colored eyes and fragile hands.

Slathering shaving cream on his face, Sam stared into the mirror and dragged his razor across his cheeks, losing himself in the feel of cold steel against his skin. And still he could feel Maggie's hand cupped in his. He hadn't expected this. Hadn't expected to find a woman who made him feel a little too much and want a little too much more.

Finished shaving, he bent his head, scooped water

over his face, then stood up and glared at his reflection. Water cascaded down his neck and ran along his chest, but he hardly noticed. His hands gripped the cold edges of the sink and he leaned his head forward until his forehead rested against the mirror.

Coming home was turning out to be even harder than he'd thought it would be.

Jeremiah waited until he heard the Jeep leave the ranch yard, its engine becoming little more than a distant purr. Just twenty minutes later Maggie's old heap of a car jumped into life, and within minutes it, too, was gone off down the road. Then, quietly, Jeremiah threw back the quilt covering him and jumped to his feet.

As he stretched the kinks out of his back and legs, he gave a low, deep-throated sigh of pure pleasure to be up and out of that bed. Saturday mornings on the ranch, he could count on one thing absolutely: Maggie would be gone for at least two hours. She'd have lunch with her friend Linda, who worked in the Curl Up and Dye hair salon, then do the grocery shopping for the week.

"Thank God Sam picked today to go visit Bert," Jeremiah muttered as he did a few deep knee bends, then touched his fingertips to his toes. "One more hour in that bed and I just *might* become an invalid."

An active man, Jeremiah hated nothing more than

sitting still. And lying down just wasn't in his game plan. A man of almost seventy knew only too well that soon enough he'd have an eternity to lie down. No point in hurrying things up any.

Grinning to himself, he hotfooted it to the bedroom door and turned the old brass key in the lock. Just in case. Then he slipped over to the bookcase, pulled down a copy of *War and Peace* and reached behind it for his secret stash.

"Ah…" He pulled out one of three cigars he had tucked away, then quickly found a match and lit it. A few puffs had him sighing in pleasure. Then, before he could forget, he walked to the bedside table and picked up the phone.

Punching in a few numbers, he puffed contentedly while he waited for his old friend to answer the phone. When he did, Jeremiah said, "Bert? Good. Wanted to warn you. Sam's headed your way."

"Damn it, Jeremiah," the good doctor complained, "I don't like this at all. Told you when you first thought it up it was a harebrained scheme, and nothing's changed."

It was an old song and Jeremiah knew the words by heart. Bert had been against this plan from the beginning. It was only their long-standing friendship that had finally convinced the doctor to go along with it.

Jeremiah tucked the cigar into the corner of his mouth and talked around it. "There's no backing out now, Bert. You signed up for this. And blast it, man, you know it was my only choice."

"Telling your grandsons you're *dying* is your only way to get 'em home?"

Jeremiah scowled into the shaft of sunlight spearing through his bedroom window. Reaching out, he lifted the sash high so that a brisk breeze flew in, dissipating the telltale cigar smoke. Did Bert think faking his own demise was a piece of cake? It sure as hell wasn't. Doing nothing but lying around sighing all day was making him sore all over. And pretending to be old and feeble irritated the hell out of him. Plus, he didn't care for the fact that he was worrying Maggie, either.

But despite how it went against the grain to admit it, the truth was there staring at him, so no point in avoiding it. "Yes, it was the only way. The boys haven't been back since…"

A long pause fell between the two old friends as they both remembered the long-ago tragedy that still haunted the Lonergan boys. Finally Bert Evans broke it with a sigh of resignation. "I know. Fine, fine. In for a penny…"

Jeremiah grinned and tried to remember where he'd stashed his spare bottle of bourbon. It might be early in the morning, but he felt as if a toast was in order. Things were moving right along according to plan.

"Thanks, Bert. I owe you."

"You surely do, you old goat."

When he hung up, Jeremiah chuckled, took a long drag of his cigar and blew a perfect smoke ring in quiet celebration.

Coleville hadn't changed much.

Sam drove down the narrow main street and let his gaze slide across familiar storefronts. Early on a Saturday morning, there were plenty of people filling the sidewalks and almost no parking spaces.

A small town, Coleville was fifty miles from Fresno, the closest "big" city. To keep its citizens happy, the town boasted a supermarket, a theater and even one of the huge national chain drugstores. And sometime over the years, Sam noted, it had also acquired one of the trendy coffee shops that were dotting nearly every corner of every street in the country.

The schools were small, as they'd always been, populated by the children who lived both in town and on the surrounding farms and ranches. And the only doctor worked out of a small clinic at the edge of town. Emergencies were handled here first and then, if needed, the patient was either driven by ambulance or airlifted into Fresno and the hospital.

Sam pulled his grandfather's Jeep into the clinic parking lot and shut off the engine. The sun blasted down on him out of a brassy sky, and he squinted at the squat building in front of him. Bert Evans, M.D.

was written across the wide window in florid gold script that was peeling at the edges. The whole place needed a good coat of paint, but there were terra-cotta tubs on either side of the double front doors overflowing with bright flowers, and the walkway and porch were swept clean and tidy as a church.

He climbed out of the Jeep, shoved the keys into his pocket and headed for the door. As he walked, memory marched with him.

He saw himself as a kid, running into the clinic and badgering Dr. Evans with hundreds of questions. The doctor had never lost patience with him. Instead he'd answered what he could and provided old medical books so that Sam could discover other things on his own.

It was in this little clinic that Sam had first decided to become a doctor. Even as a kid, he'd known he wanted to be able to fix people. To help. He'd had grand plans back then. He'd wanted to be the kind of doctor that Bert Evans was. A man who knew his patients as well as his own family. A man who was a part of the community.

Well, things changed. Now he did what he could, when he could, and tried not to get involved.

A bell over the door jangled cheerfully when he stepped into the blessed cool of air-conditioning. Three kids and their tired mother sat on the green plastic chairs in the waiting room. The mom gave him a tired smile and an absent nod while two of her kids tried to kill each other.

Behind the reception desk a young woman sat typing on a computer keyboard, and Sam flinched inwardly because he'd half expected to find Dr. Evans's old nurse still enthroned in this office. But the woman had been at least a hundred when he was a kid.

"Can I help you?" The young woman looked up from her task and gave him a smile that offered a lot more help than he required at the moment.

"I'd like to see Dr. Evans for a minute," he said. "Tell him Sam Lonergan's here."

She stood up and smoothed her hands down her pale cream-colored slacks while somehow managing to showcase her truly spectacular breasts, hidden behind a light blue sweater. "If you'll have a seat..."

He didn't, though. When she left the room, he wandered around, looking at all of the framed photos on the wall. What Dr. Evans had always called his "trophies." Babies he'd delivered, kids he'd treated, adults he'd cared for in life and seen into death. Dozens—hundreds—of faces smiled at him, but Sam only saw one.

That familiar grin slammed a well-aimed punch to Sam's gut, but he couldn't seem to look away. The boy in the photo was only sixteen—and would never get any older. Sam's hands fisted at his sides. The sounds of the squabbling kids behind him faded into nothing and he lost himself staring into the face of the one person he should have saved and hadn't.

"The doctor will see you now." A tug on his shirt-sleeve got his attention when the soft voice didn't.

"What?" He stared at the doctor's assistant, shook off the memories clouding his brain and reminded himself why he was here. "Thanks."

Without another glance at her he stalked across the room, opened the door into the back and headed down the long hallway to Dr. Evans's office. Much like the rest of the clinic, the office looked as though it had been caught in a time warp. Not a single thing was different.

The walls were still crowded with floor-to-ceiling bookshelves. There was a standing scale in one corner, and on the edge of the wide, cluttered mahogany desk, a glass jar of multicolored lollipops still stood ready for the doc's younger patients.

"Sam!" The older man leaped to his feet and came around his desk with a smile on his face. Doc Evans took Sam's hand in both of his own and shook heartily. His blue eyes were still soft and kind, but his hair was almost snow-white now. "Good to see you. Been too long, boy. Way too long."

"Yeah," Sam admitted, though it cost him another pang of guilt. "Guess it has."

"Sit down, sit down." The doctor waved a hand at the deep leather chairs opposite his desk, then took his own seat, folding his hands atop a manila file folder. "So you've been to the house? Seen your grandfather?"

"Yeah. I got in last night."

"Good, good," the older man crowed. "Then I expect you've met Maggie."

"Yes, I—"

"Fine girl, that one. Why, she's been the best medicine Jeremiah could ever ask for. Just keeps the old coot smiling all the time now." He steepled his fingertips. "Yes, she's a fine girl."

"She seems...nice," Sam said because he had to say something and he couldn't very well tell the older man that she looked great naked. Besides, he hadn't come here to talk about Maggie. In fact, Sam was doing all he could to not even think about her. So he quickly shifted the conversation back to where he wanted it. "But about my grandfather—what exactly is Pop's condition?"

Dr. Evans grumbled something unintelligible, then leaned back in his chair, stroking his chin as if he still had the beard he'd shaved off twenty years ago. "Well, now, that's, uh... You say you talked to Jeremiah?"

"Yeeesss..." Suspicion curled in Sam's mind and he narrowed his gaze on his grandfather's oldest friend. "He said that you were taking good care of him and that I shouldn't bother."

"Well, then," Dr. Evans said, trying another smile.

"Sounds like good advice to me, Sam. No point in you worrying yourself. Yessiree, it's good to see you, son."

"Uh-huh." Sam leaned in even closer to the older man, keeping their gazes locked. Didn't surprise him in the slightest when Doc Evans broke contact first, glancing first at the ceiling, then at his desk and finally settling for staring blankly out the window. "What is it you're not telling me, Doc?"

"Now, Sam," the older man whined, "you know all about doctor-patient confidentiality...."

Sam's eyes narrowed thoughtfully. "I'm not asking you to break a confidence," he said. "But as one doctor to another, you could throw me a bone here. Have you done an EKG? What're his cholesterol levels? Blood pressure? Has he had a stress test lately?"

Dr. Evans smiled and stood up, coming around the edge of his desk to pat Sam on the back as if he were a schoolboy acing his latest test. "All good questions, son. Glad to see you've become the kind of doctor I always knew you would be."

"Thanks," Sam said and let himself be nudged out of his chair and toward the door. "But you haven't really answered any of those questions and—"

"Don't you worry about a thing, Sam. Your grandpa's in good hands."

"I know that," he assured the older man. "I only wanted to—"

"Best thing for you to do," Doc Evans said,

opening the office door and ushering Sam out, "is to visit with Jeremiah. He's missed all of you."

Guilt reared up again and this time took a huge bite out of Sam. "I know. We never meant to—"

"Hell, boy," the doctor said, patting Sam's shoulder, "I know that. So does Jeremiah. But years go by and a man misses seeing his family."

"But his heart...?"

Doc Evans winced a little and glanced away. "I've been doctoring folks longer than you've been alive, Sam. Don't you worry any about Jeremiah's treatment. I'm on top of things." He gave Sam another pat, then started to close the door. "Thanks for stopping by. Good seeing you again."

Sam slapped one hand against the door, holding it open. "Why do I get the feeling you're trying to get rid of me?"

Doc Evans's blue eyes went wide and innocent behind his steel-rimmed glasses. "Why, no such thing. But I've got patients waiting for me and more in the waiting room. I'm a busy man, Sam. Busy, busy."

"Uh-huh." Sam couldn't quite put his finger on what was wrong here, but there was definitely something up. "If you don't mind, I'd like to examine my grandfather myself."

The doctor blustered a minute or two, then his features went stiff and stern. "No call for that, Sam. Don't think Jeremiah would allow that anyway. Appreciate that you're worried, boy. But you'll just have to trust me when I say things are as they should be." He swung the door closed again, pushing hard against Sam's restraining hand. "Now, if you'll excuse me…"

Sam let the door close and stood there frowning at it for a long minute before shaking his head and heading back down the hall.

Inside his office Bert Evans leaned back against the door and blew out a long breath. Dipping one hand into the pocket of his white office coat, he pulled out a handkerchief and used it to wipe his brow. Sam hadn't been fooled, he knew. But he'd done what he could.

Lying didn't come easy for Bert—mostly because he'd never been any good at it. His oldest friend, on the other hand, had a real gift for it. "Jeremiah, you old bastard," he whispered. "You really owe me for this."

Maggie walked briskly down Main Street, nodding to the people she passed, but her mind wasn't really on visiting. Which was why she was just as glad Linda had had an emergency appointment and couldn't make their standing lunch date.

Better this way, she told herself. She didn't really like leaving Jeremiah alone these days. Not when he was feeling so badly. And at that thought, her mind went to Sam and what he might be finding out from

Dr. Evans. Worry twisted inside her. Jeremiah had refused to talk to her about what he was feeling, brushing off her concern even while taking to his bed.

Frowning, she turned her thoughts from Jeremiah to Sam, and from there confusion reigned supreme. She'd known the man only twenty-four hours and already he was taking up way too much of her thoughts. But how could she not think about him?

"For heaven's sake, Maggie," she muttered, "give it a rest. You've already agreed to keep your distance. It's not like he's demanding his grandfather fire you or anything."

But he *could* if he wanted to.

A whole different kind of worry spiraled through her despite Maggie's determination to look on the bright side. It wasn't fair that she had to worry about both Jeremiah's health and her own home.

With her brain still churning, she stepped off the sidewalk and glanced around quickly before walking across the crowded supermarket parking lot. Cars came and went, but she hardly noticed. Focused on her errands, she hit the entrance and stepped into the air-conditioning with a grateful sigh. The sun was already high in the sky and blasting down with a heat that promised even higher temperatures soon.

Muzak drifted from the overhead speakers and from somewhere in the store a child's temperamental wail sounded out. Wrestling a single cart free of the others, she dropped her brown leather purse in the front section. Then she started into the produce department, muttering a curse as the front wheel of the cart wobbled and clanged with her every step.

"Do they *make* those things broken?" A deep familiar voice came from right behind her, and Maggie nearly jumped out of her sneakers.

Whipping around, she lifted her gaze—quite a bit—to look into Sam Lonergan's dark eyes. "You scared me half to death."

He shook his head, pushed her aside and curled both hands around the cart handle. "I called your name three times when you were walking in from the parking lot. Called out to you again," he said as he pushed the cart and clearly expected her to keep up, "as you were picking out this great cart."

She frowned. "I didn't hear you." She'd been too busy *thinking* about him to actually *see* him. What did that say about her?

"Clearly." He shrugged and stopped alongside the bin of romaine lettuce.

"What're you doing here?" she asked.

"Getting groceries, apparently." He bagged first one, then two heads of lettuce, then moved on to inspect the fresh green beans.

Maggie shook her head as she watched him pick through the beans carefully. "I'm perfectly capable of shopping on my own, you know."

He glanced at her. "You seem awfully territorial over a handful of green beans."

She inhaled sharply and blew the air out in a huff. Yes, she was being territorial. But this was *her* life he was intruding on. She'd been taking care of Jeremiah for two years and it sort of rubbed her the wrong way to think that he was implying in some way that she hadn't done a good job of it.

But then again, maybe getting snippy with the man wasn't the way to handle things either. "Fine," she said, congratulating herself on the calm, even tone of her voice. "We can do it together." Then she reached out and took the bag of beans from him before dumping its contents back into the bin. "And you should know, your grandfather doesn't like green beans."

He frowned, then turned toward her and shrugged again as his frown slowly faded into a half smile. "You're right. I'd forgotten. My grandmother used to make them for my cousins and I, but Pop never touched 'em."

Maggie smiled, too, and felt a whisper of something almost comfortable spin out between them. "He does like cauliflower," she suggested, in an attempt to continue the truce.

"And broccoli, too!" He laughed at the memory, and something dazzling flashed in his eyes, stealing Maggie's breath.

"You should do that more often," she said when she was sure that her voice wouldn't quiver.

"What's that?" he asked, already grabbing up a head of cauliflower and dropping it into a plastic bag.

"Smile."

He dipped his head, looked up at her, then tossed the vegetable into the basket before answering. "I just left Dr. Evan's office."

Maggie walked beside him, picking up a few lemons, a couple of grapefruits and several bunches of green onions. She didn't speak right away and she knew it was because she was afraid of what Sam was going to say. What he'd found out from the doctor.

Jeremiah hadn't spoken much about his sudden illness, and frankly she hadn't asked for information. Cowardly or not, she simply didn't want to have to face any dire truths that would have the capacity to break her heart.

"Aren't you going to ask what I found out?" He came closer and Maggie could feel the heat of his body reaching out for her.

She swallowed her own fear, told herself she couldn't hide from the truth forever and forced herself to nod. "What is it? What's wrong with him?"

"Not a clue."

"What?"

"*Excuse me.*" An overweight woman in a tight

flowered dress stared at them both. "If you don't mind, I'd like to buy some oranges."

"Sorry." Sam frowned again, took Maggie by the arm and used his free hand to guide the limping cart away a few feet. When he stopped, he released her and said, "Doc Evans wouldn't tell me anything."

"Oh, God." Maggie covered her mouth with her hand and stared up at him as terrifying thoughts wheeled through her mind. If the doctor didn't want to tell Jeremiah's grandson what was wrong with him, that could only mean the older man was desperately ill. "That can't be good. He must not want to worry you."

He folded both arms across his chest and thought about that. "Could be the reason, I suppose, but I don't think so." Shaking his head, Sam muttered, "No. There's something going on."

"What do you mean?"

"I mean," he said, "Jeremiah and Doc Evans are up to something and I want to know what it is."

Instantly defensive, Maggie said, "Are you trying to say that Jeremiah's *not* sick? Because if you are, that's ridiculous. He wouldn't do that."

"Maybe," Sam allowed, but clearly he wasn't convinced. Maggie reached for him, laying one hand on his forearm and somehow ignoring the sizzle of heat that erupted between them. "Jeremiah is a wonderful man. He would never worry his family unnecessarily. You should know that even better than I do."

He glanced down at her hand on his arm and slowly Maggie withdrew it.

"You could be right," he said finally. "But I want you to keep an eye out."

"You're asking me to *spy* on your grandfather?"

"Spy's a harsh word."

"But appropriate." Maggie shook her head and stepped out of the way as a tall man squeezed past her to get at the table full of bananas. Sam frowned, took her arm again and pushed the cart farther out of the produce section, away from most of the crowd.

He glanced around as if to make sure that no one was close enough to overhear them. Then he bent his head toward hers. "I'm not asking you to betray him. I'm only asking you to help *me*."

"Not two hours ago," she reminded him in a fast whisper, "you agreed that we should keep our distance from each other this summer. Now you're asking me to work with you against a man who's been nothing but kind to me."

He scraped one hand across his face, then grabbed her upper arms and pulled her close. She sucked in a gulp of air and held it as his face came within a breath of hers. Her heart pounded and she heard the rush of her own blood in her ears. Her gaze dropped to his mouth, then lifted to his eyes again.

"Things change, Maggie," he said, his voice low and fast. "And now I'm saying that I need your help.

I'm worried about Jeremiah. So are you." His gaze moved over her face like a caress. He licked his lips, pulled in a breath, then let her go suddenly and took a step back. "The question is, are you willing to work with me to find out what's going on around here?"

Five

Three days later an uneasy truce had been declared. She tried to stay out of Sam's way and he kept butting into her life. Okay, so the truce was only on *her* side.

The man seemed to pop up everywhere. If she was outside gardening, he showed up, leaning casually against the side of the house, watching every move she made. If she was cooking, he found his way to the kitchen, interrogating her on his grandfather's diet. If she was cleaning, he was close at hand, as though making sure she wasn't going to steal the family silver or something.

And at *all* times she felt his dark gaze on her as she would a touch.

In fact, the only time she felt as though she wasn't being watched was the evenings, spent in her own little house. But even then there was no peace. Because her dreams were full of him.

His dark eyes. His well-shaped mouth, long fingers and leanly muscled body. In dreams he did more than watch her. In dreams he held her, kissed her, tasted her, explored her body with his own and every morning she woke up just a little bit more tense than she'd been the day before.

Every nerve in her body felt as though it were on fire from the inside. There was a coiled tension within her that made every breath a labor and every heartbeat a victory.

Up to her elbows in hot, soapy water, Maggie swished the scrubbing sponge over a mixing bowl, rinsed it out, then set it carefully in the drainer. Shaking her head, she yawned, blinked tired eyes and whispered, "It's only been three days. If this keeps up, by the end of summer I'll be dead."

"What?"

She jumped, splashing a small wave of hot water onto the front of her pale pink T-shirt. When the adrenaline rush ended, she sighed, glanced down at herself, then lifted her gaze to Sam, standing in the doorway. "You have *got* to stop sneaking up on me."

A brief half smile curved one corner of his mouth, then was gone before she could get a good look at it.

"You would have heard me if you weren't talking to yourself," he pointed out.

"Right." She used the tips of her fingers to pull her wet shirt away from her abdomen, then gave it up and reached into the water for the next dish. "Before you ask," she said while she swiped a plate, rinsed it and set it to dry, "Jeremiah ate a big breakfast. Eggs. Bacon. Toast and juice."

"Cholesterol Surprise for a heart patient. Good thinking."

Turning her head to glare at him, she said, "We've been through this before. It's *turkey* bacon, egg *substitute* and *wheat* toast. Perfectly healthy."

Frowning, he walked into the room and stopped alongside her. Turning, he leaned one hip against the counter, folded his arms across his chest and said, "Sorry."

"Wow," Maggie countered. "An apology. This is so exciting."

He sighed and shook his head. "Guess I owe you more than one apology, huh?"

Turning off the rinse water, Maggie grabbed up a flowered dishcloth, dried her hands and faced him. If he was suddenly in the mood to talk, she'd take advantage of the situation.

"You've been following me around for days," she said quietly, trying to keep the ring of accusation out of her voice. "It's like you're *trying* to find something wrong with me and what I do for your grandfather. I want to know why."

Sunlight pouring in from the kitchen windows played across his features and spotlighted the worry gathered in his eyes.

"Because this is making me crazy," he admitted finally with another shake of his head. "Pop won't talk to me. Said he's got nothing to say until my cousins Cooper and Jake get here."

More Lonergan cousins to keep an eye on her. Yippee.

"When will that be?" she asked.

He pushed away from the counter, shoved his hands into his jeans pockets and walked across the room, his boot heels clacking noisily against the linoleum. "I don't know. Jake was in Spain at some road rally when the old man sent for him. And Cooper...well, he locks himself away when he's working. God knows if he's even gotten the message yet."

"I've read a couple of his books," Maggie said.

He turned to look at her. "What'd you think?"

"They terrify me," she admitted with a small smile. The last Cooper Lonergan thriller she'd read had forced her to leave her bedroom light on all night for nearly a week. The images he created were so real, so frightening, she didn't know how the man himself slept at night. "He must be one scary man— because he's got a really twisted imagination."

A sad smile raced across Sam's face. "He never used to," he said. "Cooper was always the funniest one of us. The one nothing bothered. At least until—" His voice faded away and even the echo of that smile disappeared from his eyes. "Things change."

Maggie's heart ached for him.

For all of them.

Even though a part of her wanted to shout that it had been fifteen years. Long enough to come to terms with a tragedy.

Instead, though, she only said, "You could try talking to Doc Evans again…."

He snorted a laugh. "Yeah, that'll be helpful. He just keeps muttering about doctor-patient confidentiality. No. Whatever's going on here, Jeremiah and the doc are in it together. And they're both too stubborn to break."

"Stubborn must run in your family."

"Yeah?" One dark eyebrow lifted.

"Well," she said, tossing the dish towel over her left shoulder, "you've already admitted they're not going to tell you anything and yet you don't stop trying. What's that if not stubborn?"

"Dedicated?"

She laughed and she saw a flash of appreciation dart across the surface of his eyes. And in response, a sweep of something warm and delicious rushed through her. Her hands trembled, so she pulled the dish towel off her shoulder again and wrapped it through her fingers. She pulled in a couple of short, uneasy breaths and told herself to get a grip.

"Who's that?" he asked suddenly and Maggie's head snapped up.

She looked out the kitchen window and saw one of their neighbors, Susan Bateman, rushing across the yard, her four-year-old daughter Kathleen cradled in her arms.

"It's Susan," Maggie said, already moving for the back door. "She and her family live on the ranch down the road. And something's wrong."

She threw open the door and Susan raced inside, her features taut, her blue eyes wide in a face gone pale. Blood blossomed on her white collared shirt, and the little girl in her arms whimpered plaintively. She hardly looked at Maggie, instead turning her gaze directly on Sam. "You're a doctor, aren't you?"

"Susan," Maggie said, "what—"

"I heard in town," the other woman kept talking, "that you're a doctor. You are, right?"

Sam stared at her and looked as though he wanted to deny it. But the sense of desperation clinging to Susan—not to mention Kathleen's muffled whimpering—was impossible to ignore.

"Yeah," he said tightly. "I am."

"Thank God," Susan said. "Katie cut herself on a postholer, and you were so much closer to town that I just came here right away."

At that, the little girl lifted her head from her mother's chest and turned big, watery blue eyes on Maggie and Sam. "I got a owie and it's all blooding."

"Aw, baby," Maggie cooed, stepping forward instinctively to smooth back the fringe of light blond hair on the little girl's forehead. "You'll be okay. Sam can fix it. You'll see."

She looked at Sam, mouth quivering. "Does it gonna hurt?"

Sam's mouth worked. He scraped one hand across his face and then said gruffly, "You should take her into town. She'll need a tetanus shot."

"No shots, Mommy!" The wail lifted the hairs at the back of Maggie's neck, and she winced as the child's voice hit decibels only dogs should have been able to hear.

Susan, though, ignored her child's distress and focused on reaching the doctor still staring at her. "We can take care of that later. She's hurt. She needs help *now*."

Maggie sensed his hesitation and wondered at it. She could see Sam leaning toward the girl, instinctively moving to help, but there was a distance in his eyes he couldn't hide.

"Fine," he said abruptly, and though a sense of detachment still remained in his eyes, he reached out both arms for the little girl. "Maggie," he said quickly as he examined the slice across the child's forearm, "go upstairs. There's a medical bag in my room."

"Right." She left the kitchen at a dead run and was back downstairs again a moment or two later.

He had the little girl sitting on the counter beside a now-empty sink while he carefully held her small arm under a stream of water from the faucet.

"It's still bleeding," Katie cried, kicking her heels against the wood cupboards beneath the counter.

Sam smiled at her. "That's because you have smart blood."

"I do?" She sniffled, wiped her red eyes with her free hand and stared at him.

"Yep. Your blood's cleaning your cut for us. Very smart blood."

"Mommy," she said, delighted to know how intelligent her body was, "I'm smart."

"You bet, baby girl," Susan said, watching every move Sam made.

"Here's your bag." Maggie stepped up close and set the bag down beside the little girl. Then she lifted one hand to smooth silky-soft hair off the child's cheeks.

She watched Sam, impressed and touched by his gentleness with the little girl. She'd been around him for three days now and this was the first time she'd gotten a glimpse of his heart.

"Thanks," Sam said and pulled a paper towel off the roll, gently patting the cut dry. "Katie, you just sit right here for a second and we'll fix it all up."

"'Kay."

He delved into the bag, pulled out a small package and opened it up. "These are butterfly bandages," he said as he pulled the backing off the tiny adhesive patches.

"Butterflies?" More curious now than afraid, Katie watched him as he pulled the skin of her wound together and carefully applied the bandages.

His fingers smoothed over the edges of the bandages, carefully making sure they weren't too tight, weren't pulling too closely. Then he lifted his gaze to hers and smiled into her watery eyes. "All finished," Sam said. "You were very brave."

"And *smart,*" she added with a sharp nod of her head that sent a tiny pink barrette sliding toward her forehead.

"Oh," Sam said despite the warning twinge of danger inside him, "*very* smart."

She flashed him a smile that slammed into him like a sledgehammer, and Sam had to remind himself to emotionally back up. It was the little ones that always got to him. The helpless ones. The ones with tears in their eyes and blind trust in their hearts.

At that thought, he straightened up, lifted her down from the counter and set her onto her feet.

Then he closed his bag and glanced at the child's mother. "She'll be fine. But you should still get her in to Doc Evans for that tetanus—" He broke off with a glance at the girl, then finished lamely, "For the other thing I talked about earlier."

"I will," she promised, gathering up her daughter and holding her close. "And thank you. Seriously."

"It wasn't bad," Sam assured her, uncomfortable with the admiring stares of both Susan and Maggie.

"She's my baby," the woman said, hugging the girl tightly. "Which means, everything is serious to me."

"I understand." And he did. All too well. Which was exactly why he needed the emotional distance that was, at the moment, eluding him.

When they were gone, Katie waving a final goodbye from the safety of her mother's arms, Sam felt Maggie's curiosity simmering in the air.

"You're very good with children," she said.

He forced himself to glance at her and saw the shine of interest in her eyes. Ordinarily having a woman like Maggie look at him like that would be a good thing. But not now. Not when they'd be in close quarters for the summer. Not when he'd be leaving in three months and she'd dug her own roots deep into the Lonergan ranch.

"I almost never bite," he said, choosing to make a joke out of her observation.

She tipped her head to one side and studied him.

"Jeremiah told me that you work with Doctors Without Borders."

"Sometimes," he said, trying to head her off at the pass before she started making what he did into some kind of heroics.

"And," she continued, "he said when you're not doing that, you work in hospital E.R.s around the country."

True. He kept on the move. Never staying in one place long enough to care about the people he treated. Never making the kind of connection that could only lead to pain somewhere along the line.

Frowning, Sam only said, "Jeremiah talks too much."

"What I don't understand," she said softly, keeping his attention despite the voice inside telling him to leave the room, "is why someone like you doesn't want to settle down in one place. Build a practice."

His chest tightened and his lungs felt as though they were being squeezed by a cold, invisible fist. Of course she didn't understand. The woman had been at the ranch less than two years and she'd already put her stamp on the place.

Little touches—flowers, candles—decorated the big rooms. The house always smelled of lemon oil, and every stick of furniture in the place gleamed from her careful attention. She'd nested. Put down roots here in the land that had nurtured him in his youth. Of course she couldn't comprehend why he wouldn't want the same things.

And if things had been different, he probably would have. But he'd learned early that loving, caring, only meant that you could be hurt, torn apart inside by a whim of fate. So now he chose to stand apart. To keep his heart whole by keeping it locked away.

"I like to be on the move," he said and heard the gruffness of his own voice scratching at the air. Here, in this kitchen that shone and glistened in the morning sunlight, a part of him wished things were different. Wished *he* were different.

But no amount of wishing could turn back time.

"Before," she said, apparently unwilling to let this conversation end and allow him an escape, "you told me that you weren't a nice man."

He stilled, his hands atop the medical bag that went with him everywhere. "It's the truth."

"No," she said softly. And he couldn't help it—he had to look at her.

The sun shining in behind her silhouetted and lined her form with gold. Their gazes locked. She looked deeply into his eyes, and Sam wanted to warn her that what she would see in his soul wasn't really worth a long look.

"It's not the truth at all," she was saying, her gaze on his, a small smile curving her lips. "I think you'd like to believe it's true, but it's not."

"You don't know me," Sam countered and deliberately forced himself to break the spell somehow linking them. He grabbed up his bag and took the few steps to the doorway leading out of the kitchen.

Her voice stopped him.

"Maybe not," she said quietly. "But maybe *you* don't know you very well, either."

"You shouldn't come here alone."

Maggie's rhythm was shattered and she came up out of her swim stroke to look at the man standing at the lake's edge. Under the light of a nearly full moon he looked...*amazing.*

All day she'd been thinking of him. Didn't matter that he'd managed to keep out of her way, busying himself with tasks around the ranch yard. He'd mended fences, repaired a loose board on the back porch and cleared out the empty stables where Jeremiah used to keep horses.

And when he hadn't known she was watching, Maggie had taken the opportunity to indulge herself with a good stare. He worked like a man trying to keep himself too busy to think. In the heat of the afternoon he'd stripped off his black T-shirt, and Maggie'd been mesmerized by the sight of his tanned flesh, muscles rippling with his every movement.

Heat had settled deep inside her and didn't show any signs of dissipating. She'd moved through the rest of her day in a fog of confused lust. Not that she was confused *about* the lust. That was really clear. Gorgeous man, dark, haunted eyes, deep voice, gentle hands. What woman wouldn't be tied up in knots over him?

The confusion resulted from the fact that she *knew* he wanted her, too—and was doing everything he could to avoid her. But then, hadn't they made a pact to do just that? Steer clear of each other?

So why was he here now?

Treading water, Maggie kicked her legs and waved her arms through the cool water, keeping herself afloat as she watched him. "I've been coming here alone for two years now. I'm perfectly safe."

"I came here every summer of my life. Only took the one time."

"Sam…" If they were going to have this talk, she wouldn't do it while treading water. Giving a good strong kick, she headed for shore, and as soon as the water was shallow enough, she walked across the silty bottom, sand pushing up between her toes. Water rained off her body and she wrung her hair out before tossing it over her shoulder as she moved up onto the shore, coming to a stop right in front of him.

His gaze swept up and down her quickly, thoroughly. "No more skinny-dipping?"

She glanced at the black one-piece bathing suit she

wore, then lifted her gaze to his. Smiling, she shrugged. "I'm being a little more careful these days."

Instantly the humor in his eyes disappeared and he reached for her, curling his fingers into her shoulders as he pulled her close. His eyes even darker than usual, his voice was raw. "I hope you are. You don't dive here, do you? Jump in from the ridge?"

"No," she said quickly, responding to the fear in his eyes more than to the dictatorial note in his voice. "I just come here to swim. To cool off."

She shifted her gaze to the moonlit water behind her. She tried to see it through his eyes, through the veil of a memory that clearly still shadowed him. But all she saw was the beauty. As always, being in this spot soothed her, filled her in a way that nothing else ever had. The sigh of the wind through the trees and across the open fields. The cool ripple of the water against her skin. The wash of pale light streaming down from the sky.

"It's beautiful here," she said softly, almost reverently.

"It is," he agreed almost reluctantly, his grip on her shoulders easing but not releasing. "I'd forgotten."

"Sam." She looked up at him and waited for his gaze to meet hers. "I…*know* what happened here fifteen years ago. I know why you and your cousins left and never came back."

In a heartbeat his hands tightened on her shoulders again, and she wasn't sure if he was holding on to her to keep her there or to keep himself steady.

Shaking his head, he looked down at her and sucked in a deep, long breath. "You can't know. You can't know what it's like to be so young and to lose everything."

She reached up and cupped his cheek in her palm. Heart aching for him as she saw old pain blossom in the shine of his eyes, she said, "I know what it's like to have *nothing* to lose. I know that you still have so much—but you're determined not to see it."

He pulled her even closer and loomed over her. Maggie met his gaze and wouldn't look away. The desire that had pumped inside her so fiercely came back to the forefront and made her nerve endings fire. Something fluttered in the pit of her stomach and she swallowed hard against the knot of need lodged in her throat.

"You pull at me," he admitted, his gaze sweeping over her face. "And if I could stop it, I would."

Her heartbeat galloped and her mouth went dry. "I know." She wasn't stupid. She knew it was a mistake to get involved with a man whose very presence might be a threat to her remaining at the ranch she loved. But it had been so long since she'd felt this sense of…*wanting*. And she'd *never* known the near electrical surge in her body that being close to Sam engendered.

"I've told you, I'm *not* a nice man," he said. "You have to believe me."

"I don't."

He closed his eyes and rested his forehead against hers for a heartbeat of time. Warmth spiraled through her, like ribbon falling unfettered from a spool.

"You will, Maggie," he said. "God help me, you *will* believe me."

There was that confusion again.

Then he took her mouth with his and all thought stopped. She didn't want to think. She only wanted to feel. He wrapped his arms around her, pressing her cold, wet body to his, and Maggie could have sworn she felt steam rise up between them.

When he broke the kiss, she felt bereft, unsteady on her feet and hungry for more. Every cell in her body was awake and demanding attention. She watched him swallow hard and shudder as a matching need coursed through him.

He lifted his head, stared down into her eyes and whispered, "This is a mistake."

"Probably."

"I want you," he admitted. "More than I should."

Struggling for air, Maggie smiled up at him, still stunned to her soul with the power of that kiss. "I want you, too, Sam. Mistake or not."

"Thank God."

Six

Warning bells went off in Sam's mind, clanging loudly enough that he should have reacted to them. He should have let her go, taken a huge step back and then spent the rest of the night trying to forget the taste of her. The scent of her. The feel of her.

But that wasn't going to happen.

He deepened the kiss, sweeping his tongue into her warmth, feeling the shudder that wracked her body and tasting the sigh that slipped from her mouth into his. Her arms came up around his neck, her fingers smoothing through his hair, nails dragging along his scalp. A chill raced along his spine and danced with the blood boiling in his veins.

Those warning bells came louder, but still Sam tuned them out. He couldn't walk away from this. Couldn't turn his back on a need, a hunger, that was suddenly stronger than anything he'd ever known.

A hot summer wind wrapped itself around them and Sam dived deeper into the wonder that was Maggie. Lifting her off her feet, he staggered away from the bank, laid her down on the cool, green grass and levered himself over her.

Tearing his mouth from hers, he shifted, kissing the line of her jaw, trailing his lips along the curve of her neck to the dip of her shoulder. He inhaled her scent, the lingering trace of floral shampoo in her hair, the clean, fresh scent of the lake water clinging to her skin. And he felt heat pool inside him, swamping him with a raw hunger that clawed at him.

She sighed, slid her hands up and down his back, and even through the fabric of his T-shirt he felt the warmth of her touch singeing his skin. Sam shuddered, lifted his head and stared down into eyes as dark as his own. Moonlight flashed in her eyes and highlighted the desire shining there. When she took his face between her palms and pulled him down for a kiss, her mouth met his with a tenderness he hadn't expected. A gentleness that rocked him more thoroughly than the need clamoring inside.

Then her teeth tugged at his bottom lip, her tongue

touched the tip of his and gentleness was forgotten. A nearly electrical jolt of something amazing shot through Sam, stealing his breath as it pushed his hunger to an overwhelming pitch.

He groaned and swept one hand down the length of her body, feeling every curve, enjoying the cool dampness of her bathing suit and the heat waiting for him at her center. He cupped her, and even through the fabric separating his flesh from hers, he felt that heat pulling him in. For days he'd thought about this moment. He'd dreamed about touching her, the feel of his skin against hers. The brush of her lips, the sigh of her breath.

In the few days he'd known her, Maggie had invaded his every thought. While a part of him worried over his grandfather and the consequences of returning to the ranch, there was another completely separate part of him that hadn't been able to keep from thinking about her. From the moment he'd met her there'd been *something* simmering in the air between them. Something he'd never felt before. Something he really didn't want to think about.

At the moment it was enough to have her. To touch her.

She gasped and arched into his touch, her legs separating, parting to give him easier access.

It wasn't enough.

He needed more.

Wanted more.

Still kissing him, tantalizing him, her hands dropped to his belt and tugged at his shirt, pulling the hem of it free of his jeans and then pushing it up over his chest. Her palms splayed against his skin and it felt as though she were branding him—and he wanted to feel her hands all over him.

Instantly he sat up, ripped off his shirt and tossed it to one side. He watched her and his breath strangled in his throat as she pushed first one strap of her suit, then the other off her shoulders. The tops of her breasts peeked up from the edge of the suit, straining against the stretchy fabric as if trying to escape. When she would have slid the suit farther down though, he stopped her.

Heart pounding, throat tight, he grabbed her hands, stilled them and whispered, "Let me."

She licked her lips, nodded and then closed her eyes as he pushed the bathing suit down and off her until she lay naked in the moonlight. Her tan lines gleamed pale against her honey-colored flesh, and he found himself wishing she'd worn the bikini that had created those lines.

"Went for a one-piece tonight," he murmured, lips curving.

She smiled and lifted one hand toward him. "I thought it would be…safer to be covered up, just in case I ran into you out here."

His smile faded as he watched her eyes. "Do you want to be safe?"

She shook her head. "No. I want *you.*"

"Glad to hear it." He dipped his head and took first one of her nipples and then the other into his mouth.

Her soft sighs scalded him. "Sam…"

"I've been thinking about doing this since that first night," he admitted, lifting his head as he stroked one hand down her chest, between her breasts, past her navel to the soft, dark curls at the juncture of her thighs.

"Me, too," she said and reached for him, running her fingertips down his chest, scraping her thumbnails across his flat nipples.

He groaned again, fighting for air. For control. But it was a hopeless battle. With this woman naked before him, control wasn't something he was really interested in. All he wanted, all he could think about, was burying himself inside her, feeling her heat surround him, surrendering to the hunger.

Standing up, he toed off his boots, ripped off his jeans and then knelt down on the cool, soft grass in front of her. She sucked in air like a drowning woman and reached out her arms to him.

"Don't wait," she said, planting her feet, lifting her hips and rocking them in silent invitation. "Don't wait another minute."

"No. No waiting." He stretched out over her,

bracing himself on his hands at either side of her head. His gaze locked with hers as he entered her.

"Tight."

"*Good*," she whispered, arching her head back, keeping her gaze on his as he filled her. "Oh…*Sam*…"

Better than good, he thought, biting back another groan of desperation. *Essential*. With one hard thrust he shoved himself all the way home, and she gasped, drawing her legs up, wrapping them around his hips, pulling him closer, deeper.

He rocked his hips against hers, moving in and out of her heat with a rhythm driven by an overpowering need. She moved with him in a frantic dance fed by the flames devouring them both. Together they slid into a vortex of need that erupted around them, growing even as the demands of their bodies were met. The rest of the world dropped away and it was only the two of them—wrapped in a cocoon of desire that stripped away thought, logic, caution.

Lost in the sigh of the wind and the call of a night bird, they raced toward completion. The blanket of grass their bed, the star-filled sky their roof, they were locked together in the darkness, lost in each other.

Maggie stared up into Sam's eyes as he took her, as his body claimed her, pushing her higher and faster than she'd ever been before. His body pushed into hers, and a delicious friction erupted within, sparkling through her veins like shaken champagne exploding from the bottle. She held on to him tightly, her arms and legs wrapped around his hard, strong body. She felt his breath on her cheek, saw the tempest in his eyes and knew she shared it.

Breathless, she clung to the edge of sanity and fought for the wild release just out of reach. She arched into him again and again, trying to take him even deeper inside, struggling toward the soul-shattering end waiting for her.

"Sam…Sam…" Her voice, broken, shattered the quiet.

"Come for me," he whispered, his voice rumbling through her like a freight train.

"It…feels…" She couldn't define it. Couldn't explain it. Could only enjoy it and hope she survived it. And in the next second her body splintered in a fiery burst of sensation that nearly blinded her in its raw fury. She screamed, arching into him, quivering with the slam of pleasure that rocked her right down to her soul. She trembled and held on to him as if it meant her life while wave after wave of ecstasy rippled through her again and again.

Body dissolving, a whimper clogged in her throat, Maggie still found the strength to cradle Sam when he emptied himself into her with a groan torn from the depths of his soul.

Sam lay atop her and thought that even if it had meant his life, he wouldn't be able to move. Heart thudding in his chest, he felt the rapid-fire echo of her heart beating in time with his and knew she'd been as shaken as he. Gathering his strength, he pushed himself up onto his elbows and looked down into her eyes. "You okay?"

She licked her lips, blew out a short laugh, then moaned as their bodies moved together again. "I should be fine," she said. "Once the paralysis goes away."

"I hear that." Smiling, he brushed his palm across her breast and relished the hissed intake of her breath at the contact. She squirmed beneath him, her hips twisting, and he felt his body swell within her again.

She must have felt it, too.

"I see you're not completely immobile."

"Apparently not." He rocked his hips against hers, enjoying her quick inhalation of air and the way her body responded to his intimate invasion.

Her arms dropped to her sides, then swept along the grass until they lay stretched out behind her head. She looked like an Earth goddess. Moonlight pale on her skin, the long, green grass enveloping her, her still-damp hair spread out around her, her eyes glazed with a quickening need that he felt, too.

"Maggie," he whispered, bending his head to taste her mouth, to mate her tongue with his, to give her his breath and swallow hers.

"Sam," she whispered, stretching, twisting, writhing beneath him, "we're going to do it again, aren't we?"

"Oh, yeah. *Again.*"

Sliding his hands beneath her back, he lifted her as he went to his knees. She took him deeper and groaned as she straddled him and he dropped his hands to her hips.

Throwing her head back, Maggie stared blindly up at the night sky as she rocked on him, taking him so deep inside that she felt as though he was touching the tip of her heart. Her arms wrapped around his neck. She clung to him and ground her hips against him, creating the friction that sizzled deep within.

He guided her every movement with his strong hands and held her steady even when she felt as though she were about to fly apart. Lifting her head, she looked into his eyes and dived into their darkness, drowning in their depths, losing herself in the heat, the need, the tantalizing sensations of wickedness that rippled through her and around her.

And this time when the end came hurtling toward them, they reached it together and clung to each other like survivors of a storm.

Time drifted by, and Maggie wasn't sure if minutes or hours had passed when she finally drew a deep breath and lifted her head from his shoulder. "I think that paralysis may be permanent this time."

"Better not be," he said, his voice muffled with his mouth against the base of her neck. "It gets cold out here in the middle of the night. Even in summer. We could freeze."

"Well," Maggie said, laughing slightly, "that would be embarrassing, wouldn't it? Naked ice statues discovered by some poor rancher."

He didn't respond and Maggie's smile slowly faded. Carefully he lifted her off him and she sighed with loss as his body slipped from hers. Without the sexual heat surrounding them, the kiss of the wind felt icy on her sweat-dampened skin and she shivered.

He noticed and leaned to one side, grabbed up the summer dress she'd worn over her swimsuit and handed it to her. "You should get dressed."

She frowned a little as she pulled her dress over her head and wiggled into it. Her gaze followed him as he snatched up his jeans and stepped into them, tugging them up his long, muscled legs. He buttoned them up, then turned to look down at her.

"I'm sensing the magic is over," she said and held out one hand toward him. He took it and pulled her to her feet in one smooth move.

"Maggie…" Scrubbing one hand across his face, he shook his head, bent and scooped up his T-shirt from the grass. Fisting it in one hand, he looked at her and said, "I don't want you to think that—"

"Hold that thought," she said, lifting one hand for silence and was almost surprised when she got it. "If you're going to start telling me that this—" she waved one hand at the now-flattened patch of grass "—doesn't mean anything, don't worry. I'm not expecting a proposal or something."

Her heart twisted a little. She didn't do this kind of thing lightly. She'd been with exactly one other man in her life, and then it was because she'd thought she was in love. And really, wasn't *thinking* you were in love the same as *being* in love? But even then she hadn't felt the same...*need*, that she'd felt for Sam from the beginning. Tonight had been inevitable. Where it went from here was still in question.

"Yeah, but—"

Maggie cut him off, speaking up quickly. "And you know, I don't usually sleep with a man I've known less than a week." Before he could open his mouth again, she said, "It was just..."

"I know," he said quietly. "You kind of hit me hard, too."

"Really?"

He gave her a brief one-sided smile. "You've been making me nuts for days."

"You, too," she admitted with a sigh, then clarified, "I mean, you've been getting to me, too."

"You should know," he said tightly as he pulled his T-shirt on, shoving his arms through the sleeves, "I didn't come down here tonight for this—" he paused. "I mean, that wasn't the plan."

"What was the plan then?"

"Damned if I know." He shrugged, frowned into the distance, then shifted his gaze back to hers. "Guess I wanted to see you."

"I'm glad you did."

"Me, too, but—"

"But…?"

"It's a little late to be asking," he said, "and as a doctor, I sure as hell should have known better…" He shook his head and stabbed both hands through his hair impatiently. "Can't believe I didn't think. Didn't consider—"

"What?"

He turned a flat, emotionless stare on her. "I didn't use anything." When she didn't say anything, he added, "A *condom*?"

"Oh." She thought about it for a second, then realization dawned like a hammer to the head. "Oooh."

"Crap." He closed his eyes, sighed heavily, then opened them again to look at her. "I'm guessing from your reaction that you're not on the Pill."

"No reason to be," she said and slapped one hand to her abdomen as if she could somehow protect it belatedly. "I mean, until you—tonight—well, it's been…a long time."

Oh, she really had been way too wrapped up in the heat of the moment. Her stomach did a slow swirl and dip as the ramifications of what they'd done hit home. They might have made a *baby* tonight.

"Damn it." He leaned over, grabbed his boots and straightened up again, his features tight, his eyes shuttered. "Stupid. I was stupid. Sorry doesn't seem like enough."

"We were both stupid," she reminded him. "I was there, too, so you don't get to take the whole blame. It's not as if you took advantage of me or something. I'm a grown-up and I make my own choices."

"Somehow that doesn't make this any easier."

"Maybe not," she said, "but this is just as much my fault as yours, so no point in wasting a perfectly good apology."

She tried to think. Tried to figure out where she was in her cycle. Then she gave it up because she'd never been good with math anyway. She crossed her fingers for luck and said, "I'm sure it'll be fine."

His eyes narrowed. "You're sure."

"It was only the once."

"Twice."

"Right." She blew out a breath and told herself not to panic. No point in panicking yet. She swallowed hard and nodded as if convincing herself as well as him. "It'll be fine. You'll see."

"I hope you're right," he said, his gaze still narrowed and thoughtful on her. "But you'll tell me. Either way."

"Of course," she said. "There won't be anything to tell, but if there is, I'll tell you everything."

"Good. Good." He nodded firmly, as if that settled the matter. "And just so you know, I'm healthy."

"Oh, I am, too," she assured him and wished that sex in the twenty-first century could be a little less clinical and a little more fun. Although, they'd *had* fun and now look where they were.

After that an awkward silence stretched out between them. An owl hooted in the distance, and with a push from the wind the lake lapped at the shoreline. Leaves rustled overhead, and from the next ranch came the sound of a barking dog, eerie in the darkness.

"I don't want to hurt you, Maggie," he said suddenly, his voice hardly louder than the soft, papery rustle of the leaves.

Her heart fisted in her chest and Maggie sensed him pulling even further away from her. There was misery in his eyes and a loneliness in his voice that tore at her.

"What makes you think you will?"

He shifted his gaze from her to the dark surface of the lake. He stared hard, and Maggie had the distinct impression that he was looking at the lake not as it was now but as it had been on a long-ago summer day. And almost to himself he said, "There's just no other way."

Seven

Over the next week Jeremiah sensed a change between Sam and Maggie. He couldn't put his finger on it, but he was pretty sure there was more going on between them than they were saying. Every time one of them came into the room, the other one started getting jumpy.

He was old.

Not stupid.

When his bedroom door opened, Jeremiah lay back against his pillows weakly, just in case. Sunlight lay across him in a slice of gold. He opened one eye, spotted his friend Bert and sat straight up. "About time you got here. Did you bring it?"

Bert winced and closed the bedroom door with a quiet snick. "For God's sake, keep it down. Yes, I brought it—and it's the last time," he added as he stalked toward the bed.

Bert's face was flushed, and guilt shone in his pale blue eyes so clearly it was easily readable even from behind the thick glasses he wore.

"Now, Bert," Jeremiah said, swinging his legs off the bed, "no reason to start losing your nerve now."

The other man set his black leather medical bag on the edge of the bed and gave the tarnished bronze clasp a quick twist. Then he delved one handed into the bag and pulled out a bottle of single-malt scotch. Scowling fiercely, he handed it over. "It isn't about nerve, Jeremiah. It's about what's right. I don't like lying to Sam."

Frowning himself, Jeremiah studied the bottle of scotch. "Well, come to it, neither do I. But I had to get them all home *somehow*."

"Yes, but he's here now. Tell him the truth."

"Not yet." Jeremiah shook his head and fought his own feelings of guilt. He didn't like worrying his grandsons, but once they were all here, back where they belonged, he'd tell them the truth together. Resolve strengthened, he nodded firmly and asked, "Say, Bert, when you were downstairs, did you happen to notice anything between Sam and Maggie?"

At the abrupt change of subject, Bert blinked, then

thought about it for a long minute. "Nope. Can't say that I did. Though Maggie wasn't in the house. Sam let me in." Giving his head a slow shake, he said, "Tried to talk to him about sticking around. Buying my practice."

Jeremiah perked up at that. "What'd he say?"

"Same as always," Bert said on a sigh and sat down on the edge of the mattress beside his friend. Tiny dust mites danced in the sunlight, tossed by the brush of wind slipping under the partially opened sash. "He's not staying. Not interested in sticking around. Wants to practice medicine on *his* terms."

"Disappointing," Jeremiah said on a matching sigh as he twisted the cap on the scotch bottle, breaking the seal. He lifted the bottle, took a sip, then handed it off to Bert. "The boy's a hardhead, no doubt about it."

Bert snorted, took a quick pull on the scotch and said, "Wonder where he got *that* trait?"

Maggie walked along the line, pulling the wooden clothespins free and taking down the now-dry sheets and pillowcases. Carefully she folded each item as she went and set it in the basket at her feet. When she'd finished one item, she kicked the basket along and moved on to the next.

Sam stood on the back porch, one shoulder leaning against the newel post as he watched her.

With Bert upstairs keeping Jeremiah occupied, he'd followed his instincts—which had brought him here.

To Maggie.

He didn't like admitting that, even to himself, but there it was. Without really wanting to or even trying, he'd found a connection with this woman. He was already used to seeing her every day. To hearing her sing to herself when she thought no one was around. To seeing the way she cared for his grandfather and this place.

God, he'd missed the ranch. When he was a kid, the summers he'd spent here had meant more to him than anything. This place, this ranch, had been more home to him than any of the military bases he'd grown up on. His parents had always been too wrapped up in each other to take much notice of him—so the summers with his grandparents and cousins had shone golden in his mind. He'd always known that this place was here for him. This town. This ranch.

His gaze shifted briefly away from Maggie to encompass the ranch yard. The barn/stable needed a good coat of paint, and there were a few weeds sprouting up at the edges of the building and along the fence line. In the old days, weeds had never had a chance. But times had changed.

Too much had changed.

At the thought, his gaze drifted back to Maggie. Completely oblivious to him, she kept moving along the line of clean clothes she'd pegged out to dry hours ago. She wore white shorts that hit her midthigh and a tiny yellow tank top. Her white sneakers were old and worn, and her shoulder-length dark hair was drawn back into a ponytail that swayed with her movements like a metronome.

When he found himself smiling at the picture she made, he worried.

"If you're going to stand out here anyway," she called out, never turning her head, "the least you could do is help fold."

He straightened up and blew out a disgusted breath. So much for being the stealthy type. Taking the steps to the grass, he wandered over to her side. "How'd you know I was there?"

She swiveled her head to glance at him. "I could feel you watching me."

He quirked one eyebrow at her.

She grinned briefly. "Okay, *and* I heard you come outside. The screen on the kitchen door still squeaks." Shrugging, she added, "Then there was the sound of your boot heels on the porch—not to mention that tired-old-man sigh I heard just a minute or two ago."

Her fingers never stopped. She plucked off clothespins, dropped them into a canvas sack hanging from the line and then folded the next item.

"You're too observant for your own good," he said, taking the edge of the sheet when she held it out to him.

"Oh, I am," she agreed, folding one edge of the sheet over the other, then walking toward him to make the ends meet. "Just like I've *observed* that you've been avoiding me all week."

Sunlight played on her hair, dazzling the streaks of blond intermingled with the darker strands. She squinted up at him, and he noticed for the first time that she had freckles sprinkled across the bridge of her nose. Not many. Just a few. Just enough to make a man want to count them with kisses.

Which was, he told himself, *exactly* why he'd been avoiding her all week.

Because that night with her was never far from his mind. Because with every breath he wanted her again. And again. And again.

Shaking his head, he blew out a breath. Damn it. Having her should have taken the edge off the hunger. Instead he now knew just what he could find in her arms and it was taking everything he had to keep from trying to have it again. "Like I said. Observant."

Silently he took the gathered edges of the sheet, folded them neatly and dropped them onto the stack already in the basket. When he was finished, Maggie handed him a pillowcase and took one for herself.

"Hmm," she quipped with a glance at him, "not even going to try to deny it?"

"Not much point in that, is there?"

"So want to tell me *why* you've been avoiding me?"

"Not particularly," he admitted and took the pillowcase she handed him.

"Okay, then why don't *I* tell *you?*"

"Maggie…" He dropped the pillowcase onto the stack of clean laundry.

"See," she said, cutting him off neatly, "I think you don't want to talk about that night because it *meant* something to you. And that bothers you."

He stiffened, narrowed his gaze on her and watched as she quickly plucked two more clothespins off the line, gathering up a sheet as she went. "I already told you, I don't want to hurt you."

"Yes," she said, nodding, "we've already covered that."

"So why don't we just leave it alone?"

"Can't," she said, turning to face him.

"Why am I not surprised?"

She gave him a sad smile. "Is it really so hard for you to admit that what we had that night was special?"

"No." He huffed out a breath. "It *was*. I can admit that. But I can't give you anything else."

"I didn't ask for anything else," she reminded him with a patient sigh.

"Yeah, but you will," he said, meeting her dark gaze with his own. "It's in your nature."

She laughed and the music of it slammed into him, rocking him on his heels.

"My nature," she repeated. "And you know this how?"

He waved one hand, encompassing the ranch yard, the house and *her.* "You're a nester, Maggie. Look at you. I can see the curtains you hung in the guesthouse from here. You've burrowed your way into the very place that I've been steering clear of for fifteen years."

"But you're here now."

"For the summer," he clarified, in case she'd missed him saying it in the last week. "Then I'm gone again."

"Just like that?" she asked. "You can leave again, even knowing how much your grandfather needs you? Loves you?"

Sam shifted uncomfortably. Guilt pinged around inside him like a marble in the bottom of an empty coffee can. "I can't stay," he said finally through gritted teeth.

She shook her head slowly and he followed the motion of her ponytail swinging from side to side behind her head. "Not *can't*," she said, *"won't."*

"Whichever." He sounded as irritable as he felt, but apparently the tone of his voice had no effect on her. Because she only looked at him with that same sad smile, half disappointment, half regret.

"Fine. But even if you're leaving at the end of summer, you're here *now*," she reminded him.

Yeah, he was. And he wanted her. *Bad.* For one

brief instant his body tightened and his breath staggered in his lungs. Then he came back to his senses. "You're not a 'right now' kind of woman, Maggie. And I can't make you promises."

"You keep forgetting that I didn't ask for anything from you." She stepped toward him, cupped his cheek in her palm and stared directly into his eyes. "What? Only men are allowed brief, red-hot affairs?"

He caught her hand in his, stilling the feel of her fingertips against his skin. "What about the other?"

"Hmm?"

"The chance of pregnancy?" Couldn't believe he had to remind her about *that*.

Realization dawned on her features, but she said, "I don't know yet. But since there's nothing we can do about it at the moment, no point in worrying about that until we know for sure, is there?"

"Guess not." Though he knew damn well a corner of his mind would be worrying about that small chance nonstop until he knew one way or the other.

"And we could be careful."

Her voice brought him back from his thoughts, and as he looked down into her eyes, he felt his resolution to keep his distance fading into nothingness. If they were careful, if she didn't expect more from him than he could give…

It would be crazy.

Stupid.

Great.

When he didn't speak, she shrugged. "Either way," she mused, still giving him that half smile, "still got to get the laundry in."

With the abrupt shift in subject, Sam felt as if he'd just been shown a safe path through a minefield. As she walked along the line to take down the next sheet, he studied the sway of her hips, despite knowing that he'd be better off ignoring it. "Why don't you just use the dryer on the service porch?"

"This way things smell better," she said, lifting one shoulder in a half shrug as she reached up to the line. The hem of her tank top pulled up, displaying an inch or two of taut, tanned abdomen. Just enough to tempt him. "The wind and the sun...at night, you can sleep on sheets that make you dream of summer."

That'd be good, he thought, shoving his hands into his jeans pockets. But then, *anything* would beat the kind of dreams he normally had.

"Besides," she was saying as she tossed him one end of a pink-and-blue floral sheet, "when I was a little girl, I always wanted my own clothesline."

He chuckled, surprising both of them. "That's different."

She glanced at him, then looked down at the sheet they were folding. "There was a house down the street from where I lived and this woman would be out there almost every day." Her voice went soft and hazy and he knew she was looking at a memory. "She had this big golden dog who followed her all around the yard and she'd laugh at him while she hung out clothes to dry. Sometimes," she added, smiling now, "her kids would go out there, too. And they'd all play peek-a-boo in the clean clothes and it all looked so...*nice*."

"So your own mom wasn't the clothesline type, huh?"

Maggie's features stiffened and a shutter dropped over her eyes. "I don't know what my mother preferred," she said and heard the wistfulness in her voice. "I never knew her."

She glanced at Sam and saw his wince. "Sorry."

She shrugged again and reached to push up the strap of her tank top that had slid down her arm. "Not your fault. You didn't know."

"And your father?"

She forced a smile. "He's a mystery, too. They died when I was a kid. I went into the system and stayed there until I was eighteen. That neighbor I told you about? She lived down the street from the group home."

"You weren't adopted?"

"Nope. Most people want babies. But don't get that sympathy look on your face," Maggie warned. She hadn't needed anyone's pity in a long time and she sure didn't want it from Sam. "I did *fine*. There were a couple of foster parents along the way and the group home was a good one." Wanting to throw up roadblocks on memory lane, she changed the subject fast. "Anyway, now that there's a clothesline nearby, I get to indulge myself."

Thankfully he didn't ask anything else about her childhood. It hadn't all been popcorn and cotton candy, but it hadn't exactly been a miserable Dickensian childhood or anything, either. But that was the past and she had the present and future to think about.

"Indulge yourself even though this way it's more work."

"Sometimes more work makes things better."

"Not your average attitude these days."

She smiled at him. "Who wants to be average?"

"Good point." He finished folding the sheet, glanced around the yard. "You know, there's something still missing from your laundry recreation. Pop used to have a dog."

"Bigfoot." Maggie nodded sadly. "I know. He died last year."

"Last year?" Sam whistled as he did the math. "He had to have been nearly twenty years old."

"Almost," Maggie agreed, "and pretty spry right up to the end. Jeremiah was brokenhearted when that dog died. He said it was his last link to you and your cousins."

He slapped one hand to his chest and rubbed it hard, as if her words had hit him like a dart.

"You shouldn't have stayed away so long," she said.

His gaze slid to hers. "I couldn't come back. Couldn't be here…be surrounded with memories. Couldn't do it."

"But you're doing it *now*."

He snorted. "Just barely."

"Maybe it'll get easier the longer you're here."

"No, it won't."

"You could try. For *his* sake." She nodded in the direction of the house.

"It's only for *his* sake that I'm here at all." He reached up, closed one hand around the nylon clothesline and hung on as if it were a life rope tossed into a stormy sea.

"It wasn't your fault." She said it without thinking, and the minute those words came blundering out of her mouth, Maggie knew they'd been a mistake.

His features froze over. His jaw clenched. She watched him grind his teeth together hard enough to turn them to powder. And his gaze—dark, filled with pain—stabbed hers. "You don't know anything about it."

"You could talk about it. Tell me."

Another harsh, rasping laugh shot from his throat as he shook his head. "Talking about it doesn't change anything. Talking about it doesn't help. It just brings it all back."

"Sam," Maggie said softly, "you don't *have* to bring it back. It's with you all the time."

"God, I know that." He blew out a breath, seemed to steady himself, then started talking again, forcing a change of subject. "So how'd you come to be here on the Lonergan ranch, working for Jeremiah?"

Maggie nodded, silently agreeing to the shift in topic, and she was pretty sure she caught the flash of relief in his dark eyes. Then she took down the next sheet and handed one end to him. They had a rhythm now, working together as a team, and a part of her wished that that teamwork could spill over into other areas.

"My car broke down," she said. "Right outside the front gates." Pausing to remember, she added, "*Broke down* doesn't really cover it. More like it fell apart."

One corner of his mouth lifted and Maggie wondered what he looked like when he was *really* smiling. Or laughing.

"Anyway," she said, getting her mind back on track, "Jeremiah invited me in, made me lunch, called a mechanic. And by the time Arthur's Towing Service arrived to take my car away to heap heaven, your grandfather had offered me a job as his housekeeper."

"That explains how you got here," he agreed, folding the sheet and setting it down on top of the rest. "Now tell me why you're *still* here."

Nodding, Maggie straightened up and looked around beyond the ranch yard and the outbuildings. To the now golden-brown fields stretching out for miles all around them, the acres of blue sky overhead and finally to their closest neighbor, the Bateman ranch house that was no more than a faint smudge of red in the distance.

Finally she looked back at him. "Why wouldn't I be?" she asked. "It's beautiful here. I like the small town. I love your grandfather—and I owe him a lot. He gave me a place to belong."

A simple word and yet it meant so much to Maggie. It probably meant more than Sam would ever be able to truly understand. No one who'd had a home and a family could ever really know how lonely it was to be without those things.

"And," she said, "working for Jeremiah gives me plenty of time to take classes at the community college in Fresno."

"What kind of classes?"

"Nursing. I…*like* taking care of people."

"According to Jeremiah and Doc Evans, you're good at it, too."

"Thanks."

"You're welcome."

The conversation was dwindling pretty fast. But maybe that was because they were through working. There was nothing else to focus on but themselves. Each other.

Afternoon sunlight streamed down from a brassy sky, and heat radiated up from the pebble-strewn dirt. A halfhearted puff of wind stirred things up a bit without cooling them off.

And seconds continued to tick past.

He looked down at her, a thoughtful expression on his face, and Maggie wondered just what he was thinking.

More than that, she wondered if he was ever going to kiss her again. Heartbeat suddenly thundering in her ears, she was painfully aware of every shallow breath panting in and out of her lungs. Her mouth was dry, her throat tight.

He continued to stare at her. His dark, shadow-filled eyes drew her in. She couldn't have looked away even if the notion had occurred to her. There was something about this man that touched something in her no one else had ever come close to.

And, oh, God, she wanted his mouth on hers again.

As if he were reading her mind, his gaze dropped briefly, hungrily, to her mouth. Maggie's stomach did a nose dive and heat pooled somewhere even farther south.

When he reached for her, she leaned in toward him, and her breath caught as his hands closed around her upper arms.

Lowering his head to hers, he whispered, "We're going to make the same mistake again, aren't we?"

She felt his breath on her face and nearly sighed. Then, looking deeply into his eyes, she said, "Every chance we get."

Eight

His mouth came down on hers and Maggie felt herself sway into him. Her breasts pressed against his broad chest, her nipples hardened in eager anticipation.

Her lips parted under his and his tongue swept inside. She sighed and gave herself up to the intense sensations pouring through her. Deliberately she shut her brain down and ignored completely the one small, rational voice still whispering warnings in her brain.

He pulled her even tighter against him, and the combined heat from his body and the blistering warmth from the afternoon sun on her back made Maggie feel as though she were about to combust.

He growled low in his throat, and one of his hands

slid down her spine to the curve of her rear. He held her tightly to him until she felt his erection through the thick fabric of his jeans. Instantly her own body went hot and needy.

She wrapped her arms around his neck and clung to him, and when he tore his mouth from hers to lavish kisses along the length of her throat, she threw her head back and stared blindly at the clear summer sky overhead. There was a delicious haze at the edges of her vision and a distinct wobbly feel to her knees.

And she was loving every minute.

"Well. Ahem." A deep voice, then a cough, then someone said, "Excuse me, I didn't mean to interrupt."

Oops!

Abruptly the moment was shattered. Maggie swayed unsteadily as Sam lifted his head to reluctantly face the speaker. Doc Evans stood on the back porch, studiously avoiding looking at them by using his handkerchief to polish the lenses of his glasses.

"Hi, Doc." Sam took a step back from Maggie, though it cost him. His body was tight and hard and his vision was blurred with the desire nearly throttling him. Beside him Maggie quickly tugged the hem of her tank top down and ran one hand over the sides of her head, checking to make sure her ponytail was still straight.

"Just wanted to let Sam know I was leaving," the doc said, slipping on his glasses and stuffing the handkerchief into his pocket.

"How is Jeremiah feeling?" Maggie asked, and if her voice sounded a little breathless, Sam was probably the only one to notice.

Doc took the few steps to the yard and glanced at the watch on his left wrist before answering. "He seems…better."

Sam's eyes narrowed on the older man. With lust still pounding through his blood, he was on the ragged edge of control. This thing with his grandfather—the unidentified "illness"—was bothering him, and now seemed like as good a time as any to have some questions answered. "Have you determined just what the problem is yet?"

"Not yet. Um, still running a few tests…" He started rocking on his heels and his gaze shifted to a spot just to one side of Sam. "I'll, um, keep on top of things, though. Don't you worry."

"Doc…" Every instinct he had was telling Sam that something was definitely up. Bert Evans and Jeremiah had been best friends and fishing buddies most of their lives. There wasn't much one wouldn't do for the other. Up to and including trying to pull a fast one. He crossed the yard to the other man and looked down at him. "Is there something I should know?"

Doc ran one finger along the inside of the collar of his shirt and swallowed hard. Still not meeting Sam's gaze, he shook his head. "Nope, not a thing, boy. Everything's as it should be."

"Uh-huh." Folding his arms over his chest, Sam braced his feet wide apart and simply stood there. Waiting.

Seconds ticked past, and a strong breeze jumped up out of nowhere and rushed through the yard. The older man shifted uneasily on his feet, glanced around the yard, looking everywhere but at Sam.

"He's faking, isn't he?"

Bert's gaze snapped to his and he didn't even have to say anything for Sam to know that he'd guessed right. Guilt was stamped on the other man's features.

"Now why would you say that?" The doctor asked, deliberately avoiding answering the question outright.

"Because," Sam said, scowling now, "it occurs to me that if Jeremiah was really as desperately ill as you two want me to think, you'd have him in the hospital. Or at the very least, have a trained nurse here taking care of him."

"Maggie's here," Doc argued.

"Yes," Sam said and heard Maggie come up to stand beside him. "And she's been great with Pop. But she's not a trained nurse. Not yet anyway," he conceded, remembering that she was studying to be just that. "So I have to wonder, Doc. Is Jeremiah putting one over on me? Or *you?*"

The older man cleared his throat, rubbed his jaw, then blew out a breath. When he didn't speak, Maggie did.

"Dr. Evans," she said, aligning herself with Sam, "is Jeremiah ill or not?"

He huffed out another breath, swallowed hard, then admitted, "I never wanted to lie to you, Maggie. Or you either, Sam."

"I don't believe this," Maggie muttered.

"I do," Sam said with a shake of his head. "The old goat tricked us into coming home."

Instantly Bert's eyes fired up and his spine straightened as if someone had suddenly shoved a steel pole down the back of his shirt. Shaking an index finger at Sam as if he were still a kid and needed a good dressing-down, the older man said, "It's a damn shame that old goat *had* to trick the three of you into coming back to the ranch." He took a breath and rushed right on before Sam could try to defend himself. "You boys haven't been back since that summer, and do you think that's right? Do you think it's a fair thing to do? Cutting your grandfather out of your life?"

"No, but—" Sam shoved both hands into his pockets and backed up a step. He also noticed that Maggie's gaze was on him.

"There's no buts about it, boy," Doc Evans said. "You three mean the world to that 'old goat' in there. Not surprising he'd do whatever he had to do to get you back here, now is it?"

No, it wasn't. And if the doc's aim had been to

make Sam ashamed of himself, it had worked. But no one could understand just how hard it was to come back to Coleville. To this place that had once meant everything to him. No one could know that coming here, being here, felt as if he was somehow dismissing what had happened that summer. As if he was trying to forget.

"It was an accident," Doc said, his voice softer now. "But you three have been making Jeremiah pay in loneliness. That isn't right."

Sam didn't trust himself to speak. Guilt roared through him with a sound so thunderous it surprised the hell out of him that the others couldn't hear it. The doc was right. Jeremiah had been punished for something that wasn't his fault. Sam and his cousins had each cut this ranch and the old man out of their lives to make living with that summer easier on *themselves*. But they'd never stopped to consider how their actions affected their grandfather. And what kind of bastards did that make them?

He scrubbed one hand over his face and turned away, suddenly unable to face the accusatory glare in Doc Evans's eyes. He walked across the yard in long, hurried strides until he reached the edge of the field. Then he stopped and stared. Stretched out for miles in front of him, open land raced toward the horizon. The breeze whistled past him, lifting his hair, tossing dirt into his eyes. Midday sun beat down on him like a fist and made him feel as though he were standing at the gates of hell, feeling the heat reaching out for him.

Appropriate.

Behind him, he absently listened to Maggie thanking Bert for coming and then to the soft sounds of the doctor's footsteps as he left. Shame still rippled inside Sam and he had no defense against it. The bottom line was he and his cousins had forced their grandfather into faking a serious illness just to get them home.

"Are you okay?"

Maggie came up beside him and laid one hand on his arm. The simple heat of her touch, the gentleness of her voice, eased back the knot of pain lodged in the center of his chest.

"No," he admitted, never taking his gaze from the horizon. "I don't think I am."

She sighed. "What Jeremiah did wasn't right. He shouldn't have worried you and your cousins—or me."

Finally then Sam looked at her, caught the worry in her dark eyes and warmed himself with it. "He shouldn't have worried *you*. *We* had it coming."

"You're being really hard on yourself."

He laughed at that. "Aren't you the one who's been telling me that I should never have stayed away?"

"Yes," she said. "But if anyone should have understood what you were feeling, it should have been Jeremiah."

"No." Sam turned to face her and laid both hands on her shoulders. "He couldn't. Because he doesn't know all of it."

"Tell me," she said, reaching up to cover his hands with her own. "Tell me what happened."

His fingers tightened on her shoulders, his grip clenching as if holding on to her to steady himself. Maggie sensed the pain radiating from him and wished she could do something to ease it. But there was nothing—not unless he could talk to her. Tell her what it was that kept him in pain. Kept him from the home and the grandfather that he loved.

"Sam…"

He inhaled sharply, deeply, and blew the air out again in a rush. "Every summer we came here. There were four of us. All of us born within a year or two of each other. Our fathers were brothers and we were more like brothers than cousins ourselves."

His eyes misted, and she knew he was staring into the past, not seeing her at all, though his grip on her shoulders remained strong.

"Me, Cooper, Jake and Mac." A wistful smile curved one corner of his mouth. "I was the oldest, Mac the youngest. Not that it mattered," he admitted.

The wind kicked up again, twisting dirt into tiny tornadoes that raced across the yard in front of them.

"Mac was brilliant. Seriously smart. He was only sixteen, but he had some great ideas." Sam smiled now and Maggie felt the tension in him climb. As if talking about that last summer brought it all even closer. "That year Mac had come up with some gizmo he said would make us all rich."

"Really?" Maggie smiled up at him, trying to make this easier. "What was it?"

He smiled back at her and shook his head. "Hell if I know. Mac and Jake were big into motorcycles, though—always tinkering with some damn thing or another. And that summer the two of them said they'd come up with something that was going to improve engine performance and make us all millionaires." His smile faded slowly. "They were right. The royalties on that invention have been incredible. But Mac never lived to see them."

"Tell me what happened."

He let her go and shoved both hands through his hair as he took a step back. Distancing himself from her? Or from the memories gathering around him?

"It was a contest," he said bitterly, his mouth twisting as if even the words had a foul taste. "We took turns jumping off the ridge into the lake. We got 'points' both for how far out we were able to jump and for how long we stayed underwater before surfacing."

Maggie's stomach fisted and sympathy washed through her. She reached for him, but he shook his head.

"Just…let me get it out." He swallowed hard and

stared off into the distance again, seeing the past unroll in front of him. "It was Mac's turn. Jake had already outjumped all of us." A choked-off laugh grumbled from his throat. "Mac hated to lose. He took a running start, jumped off the ridge and landed farther out than any of us had gone before. Jake was pissed, but to win, Mac had to stay down longer than he had, too."

"Oh, God…" She knew what was coming. Knew that Mac had died that long-ago summer day and, in dying, had set his cousins on a path that had kept them from everything they'd ever cared about.

Sam kept talking as if Maggie hadn't spoken. "I was timing him. Had Jeremiah's stopwatch. Mac had been under two minutes when I started worrying."

"Two minutes? Isn't that an awfully long time?"

"Not for him. He'd done it before. But this time…" Sam shook his head. "It felt…different. Don't know why. I told Cooper we should go in after him, but Cooper wanted Mac to beat Jake, so he said to give him another few seconds. We waited. We should have gone in after him, but we waited." His eyes filled with tears that he viciously rubbed away a moment later. "Not *we*. *Me*. *I* should have gone in after him. I knew something was wrong. Knew he was in trouble. *Felt* it. But I waited."

"Sam…" Her heart ached for him. For the pain he'd carried for so long.

"I waited, stood there on the ridge *timing* him, for God's sake, while Mac was dying."

"You're being too hard on yourself. You always have been."

He snapped her a furious glare. "Weren't you listening? I *knew* he was in trouble."

"You had a bad feeling. You were a kid, too."

He brushed off her attempt at understanding and said, "I was the oldest. I should have known better. It was *stupid* to jump off that damn ridge. At two minutes and fifteen seconds, I couldn't take it anymore. I ran and jumped in. The others were right behind me. The lake water was cloudy." He squinted, as if still trying to see his cousin through the murky water. "Took us too long to find him. Took *forever.* He was lying on the bottom. We grabbed him and dragged him out. Laid him on the bank and pushed the water out of him, but it was too late. He was dead. Mac was dead."

She reached for him, taking hold of his forearm, and his tensed muscles felt like steel beneath her palms. "I'm so sorry, Sam. But it wasn't your fault."

"That's what everybody said," he told her on a sigh. "Doc Evans examined the…body. He said Mac broke his neck when he jumped in—and unconscious, he drowned. And after that nothing was ever the same again."

"You stayed away, Sam," she said, sensing somehow that he didn't want her sympathy now any more than he had before. "You made that choice. You and the others. You didn't have to. No one blamed you."

"*I* blamed me. Mac *drowned*. While we all stood there, *timing* him, he *died*."

"You're not psychic, Sam. You couldn't have known that he broke his neck."

He shook his head, refusing to hear her. Refusing to drop the burden of guilt he'd been carrying so long it had become a part of him. "I should have known he was in trouble. If I'd gone in when I first wanted to, I could have saved him."

"He broke his neck," she reminded him softly.

"He was only sixteen."

"I know…" She lifted one hand and laid her palm against his chest, feeling the thundering beat of his heart. "But does staying away from Coleville make it easier?"

"Nothing makes it easier."

"Then why stay away? Couldn't you—I don't know—honor Mac's memory by coming home? Being the doctor this town needs? By living your life and being happy?"

Hope flickered briefly in his eyes before fading away again. God, Sam would like nothing better than to agree with her. To tell her yes, he'd stay. He'd stay here in Coleville, move back to the ranch. Surround himself with everything he'd missed for so long.

But he couldn't.

He'd failed Mac.

And now he wasn't *allowed* to be happy.

She frowned up at him and he saw the disappointment in her eyes when she asked, "Do you really think Mac would want you all to be miserable for the rest of your lives? To avoid coming home to the place you all loved so much?"

"No, he wouldn't," he said softly, reaching out to run the tip of his fingers along her cheek. "But that doesn't seem to matter. Not for me. Or the others."

"So when the summer's over, you'll leave again."

He swallowed hard. "Yes."

"And not come back."

"Yes."

"No matter how far you run, Sam," she said quietly, "you'll never be able to outrun your past. I know. I've tried."

Nine

"Mad at me, aren't you?"

Maggie turned from the chest of drawers where she was putting away the old man's clean laundry to stare at him. He looked worried. And as guilty as a child who'd stolen a cookie just before dinner.

Her heart turned over and she realized that as disappointed as she'd been in him that he'd lied to her—she was more relieved to know that he wasn't sick at all. He'd become so important to her over the last two years. This one old man had become the family she'd always longed for, and the thought of losing him had terrified her.

"Mad?" she repeated with a slow shake of her

head. "No, not now. But I *was*. When Doc Evans first told us the truth."

"I'm real sorry about that, Maggie," Jeremiah said and hung his head before glancing up at her from beneath bushy gray brows. "Didn't like lying to you, if that's any comfort."

His gray whiskers shone in the late afternoon sunlight streaming through his bedroom window. Wisps of gray hair fluttered around his head in the breeze dancing under the partially opened window. And his dark eyes glittered with the hope that he was forgiven.

Love filled her, sweet and rich, and Maggie knew she couldn't hold out against him. Smiling at him, she said, "I'm just glad you're not really sick, Jeremiah. You had me scared."

He winced and hunched his shoulders as he pushed himself off the bed and stood up. "I'm sorry about that, too, girl. It's just…I couldn't think of any other way to get my boys home."

In a weird way, she understood the desperation of his lie. But still. "You worried everyone."

"I know."

"Sam's pretty angry."

He sighed. "I figured he would be." Then, nodding, he added, "But he's *here*. That's the important thing. And he'll stay the summer. Just as the others will. They all gave me their word."

"What made you do it, Jeremiah? I mean, I know you miss them. But why now? Why *this* summer?"

He smiled again, and this time she saw that he was enjoying being secretive. "Can't tell you that yet, Maggie. I'm going to wait until all of my boys are home to spill that secret."

"You're as stubborn as Sam," she said with a slow shake of her head. Turning, she went back to the dresser and carefully stacked clean T-shirts in the top drawer.

"You like him, don't you?"

She narrowed her eyes and glanced at him over her shoulder. "Jeremiah…"

He held up both hands and grinned. "Just asking. I've been watching the two of you—and I'm not so old I can't see the sparks flare up when you're together."

She flushed and hoped he hadn't sensed just how hot those sparks had gotten. Her heartbeat quickened and heat pooled deep in her center just thinking about the single night she'd had with Sam. And it wasn't just the amazing lovemaking—it was watching him with Jeremiah, seeing him help little Katie. Seeing his tenderness and aching at his loneliness. He touched her in so many ways, but… "It doesn't matter, Jeremiah. He's still leaving."

"And you're going to let him?"

Her gaze snapped up to his. "It's not up to me, Jeremiah. You know that. Sam told me. About Mac."

The old man slumped as if someone had let the air out of his body. "It was a terrible thing, no doubt," he said, his voice a low rumble. "But it's time they all came to grips with it. Learned to let Mac go."

"I don't know if Sam can," Maggie whispered, remembering the shadows in his eyes when he'd told her the story of that summer day.

"I hope you're wrong about that, Maggie."

Hours later Sam stared out the kitchen window at Maggie's house across the yard. The summer night was clear and bright under the light of a full moon. A wind swept across the fields and rattled the leaves of the trees, sounding like a whispering crowd making bets on whether or not Sam would be able to stay away from Maggie.

Hell, even he wouldn't take that bet.

From the living room came the sound of the television, some game show with a too-enthusiastic host shouting at a contestant. Jeremiah, now that his pretense of illness was over, lay comfortably in his recliner, snoozing.

Sam frowned and shoved both hands into his jeans pockets. He'd had it out with Jeremiah before dinner, telling his grandfather just what a rotten thing he'd done by pretending to be dying. By worrying them all.

But after apologizing, Jeremiah had said in his own defense, *I'm sorry to hurt you, boy, but the day that Mac died, I didn't lose one grandson—I lost four. Can't blame me for trying to get 'em back.*

And the truth was, Sam couldn't blame him. Couldn't even be angry about being tricked into coming home. Because honestly he'd missed this ranch and that cranky old man more than he could ever say.

Opening the back door, Sam stepped out onto the porch and closed the door behind him, shutting out the drone of the television and the rumble of Jeremiah's snores. The summer night was warm, but the breeze sweeping across the open fields was cool enough. The scents of his childhood wrapped themselves around him, and he closed his eyes just to concentrate on them. Summer grass, clean, sweet air and from some-where—probably the neighboring ranch—he caught the distinct aroma of steaks on a barbecue.

A low growl in the distance announced approaching thunder and the promise of rain sometime soon. He glanced up at the sky and watched as massive dark clouds rolled in from the coast, obliterating the moon, covering the ranch yard in deep shadow. How many storms, he wondered, had he and his cousins watched from the safety of this old porch? How many nights had they sat out here with cold sodas, watching lightning dance across the sky while they talked about girls and school and cars and every other subject so important to teenage boys? They'd all been so close. So much a part of each other.

So when Mac died, his leaving had splintered the rest of them. They hadn't known how to talk to each other anymore. There were only three of them. They were off balance. Out of sync. Like a three-legged dog trying to remember how to run, they'd stumbled and fallen and finally they'd quit trying.

A shimmer of lightning flashed behind the clouds, illuminating them briefly just before a clap of thunder rattled the window glass in the door behind him.

Sam leaned one shoulder against a porch post and shoved both hands into his jeans pockets as he shifted his gaze back to Maggie's house. It was taking everything he had in him to keep from crossing the yard, knocking on that door and begging her to let him in.

He'd been on his own for years—but he'd never been as *alone* as he was at that moment.

And for the first time in far too long, he hated it.

Across the yard Maggie's front door opened and a slice of lamplight stretched across the ground, reaching for him. She held the screen open and stepped outside. "Are you going to stay there all night?"

His heart gave one sudden hard jolt against his chest. "I was thinking about it."

She tipped her head up, glanced at the sky, then lowered her gaze to him again. "Looks like rain."

Thunder growled in the background as another flash of light shattered the dark.

"Looks like," he agreed, though he couldn't tear

his gaze from her long enough to look at the sky. She stood like a dancer, all fluid grace. Then she moved, taking another step toward the edge of her porch, letting the screen door swish shut behind her. Backlit, she looked like a dream, gilded curves and long hair loose around her shoulders.

"You'll get wet if you just stand there."

Nature's cold shower.

Not a bad idea.

But he only said, "Probably."

"It's better in here."

"But not safer," he pointed out. Though the thought of going to her, letting himself be surrounded by her warmth, was nearly enough to bring him to his knees.

"Are you so concerned with being safe?" she asked.

"I'm trying to be," Sam said. "For your sake."

She tipped her head to one side and her hair swung in a lazy arc. "And you said you're not a nice man."

"I'm not. I'm really not."

Overhead, lightning cracked and white-hot light pulsed over the yard. Thunder boomed, deafening, and the echo of it rolled through Sam until he felt his whole body shaking with it.

"I don't believe you."

"Damn it." He muttered the words as he jumped off the back porch. Frustration punched at him. Couldn't she see what it was costing him to try to do the right thing? His boots hit the dirt just as the first fat drops of warm rain splattered from the sky. He hardly noticed. His long legs carried him across the yard in a few hurried strides. He stopped at the foot of her front porch steps and stared up at her. "I'm trying like hell to stay away from you, Maggie."

She smiled. "Who asked you to?"

"*You* should be."

"See, I don't think so."

He looked up into her dark eyes while the lightning lit up the yard like a strobe light in a crowded club, and the emotions flashing in her eyes were just as wild. Just as dangerous.

"I think you're a better man than you pretend to be."

He pushed one hand through his hair, wiping the rain back and out of his eyes at the same time. "That's because you don't know me."

"Oh, I think I do," she said. "For instance, I know you volunteer with Doctors Without Borders— helping children who desperately need it."

"Because I can help them and leave," he said flatly, refusing the halo she kept trying to fit him for. "It's not noble, it's *safe*." Rain slapped at him, thunder boomed and lightning flashed. He stared up at her, rain falling into his eyes and trailing down his face like hot tears. "I do my job and then I leave. I don't hang around. Don't make friends. Don't *care*."

"Yes, you do. You care," she said stubbornly and

he wondered why in the hell she wouldn't listen. Wouldn't run. "You care more than you want to."

"You're wrong," he insisted. "I travel around the country, work different E.R.s for a couple months and then leave. I don't stay, Maggie. Not anywhere. I won't get involved again. Won't *care*. It's the only way to keep from getting my heart ripped out. Again."

She reached out to him, her fingers trailing over his cheek, wiping away the rain and smoothing his wet hair back from his face. "If you have to protect yourself, go ahead. But you don't have to protect me from you, Sam. I'm a big girl. I make my own choices."

"If you had any sense," he muttered thickly, "you'd tell me to get the hell away from you."

She smiled and shook her head. "Now, why would I do that when I so much want you to stay?"

He flinched. "I can't. Stay I mean. Don't count on that, Maggie."

She came down the steps and into his arms, wrapping her own arms around his neck and looking into his eyes. She said softly, "I meant stay *tonight,* Sam. Stay with me tonight."

The heat of her body sank into him, warming all the cold, dark places inside him. The scent of her— shampoo, soap and *woman*—filled him and Sam knew he couldn't leave. Not even for *her* sake.

He pulled her close, his gaze moving over her face like a touch. And when he couldn't stand waiting another moment, he took her mouth with his, parting her lips with his tongue, sweeping inside, tasting her, exploring her. He claimed her breath and gave her his own. He slid one hand up her spine and into her hair, threading his fingers through the thick, soft mass and holding her head still for his conquest.

She sighed and melted into him and the rain pelted them both. Thunder and lightning rattled the sky. The wind howled. And neither of them noticed. His heartbeat roared in his chest and his blood pumped fierce and wild.

He took her deeper, harder, and felt her arms tighten around his neck as she gave herself up to him. Again and again he plundered her mouth hungrily, eagerly, until finally, needing air, he tore his mouth from hers and moved to taste the length of her throat. His lips trailed heat up and down that long, slender column, and she shivered in his grasp, moaning gently and tilting her head to one side to grant him easier access.

It wasn't enough.

Would never be enough.

Groaning tightly, he pulled back long enough to scoop her into his arms. Then he stepped up onto the porch, opened the screen door and walked inside. Holding her close, he kicked the door closed and stalked across her cozy living room to the bedroom.

He knew this house as well as he knew the main

house. When he was a kid, the foreman had lived here and he and his cousins had run free through the place.

It had changed, of course, which he absently noticed as he headed for her bedroom. Soft colors on the wall, framed posters of faraway countries and, over it all, the scent of flowers and fresh coffee.

She nibbled at his neck and Sam groaned again, his body fisting, his breath laboring. He crossed the short hall and entered the only bedroom. The mattress was covered by a quilt and the edges had been turned down, as if she'd prepared it for them. He could only be grateful.

Standing her on her own two feet, he took a step back from her and yanked off his sodden T-shirt. "I need you, Maggie. Here. Now. I need you."

Her lips curved in a self-satisfied smile as she pulled her tank top up and off. She wasn't wearing a bra. His hands itched to cup her breasts. But she walked up to him and pressed herself against him, her hardened nipples branding his bare chest with twin points of heat.

He dropped his head to the curve of her neck and feasted on her smooth skin. With lips, tongue, teeth, he tasted her and felt the shivering reaction ripple through her as she sighed.

Maggie leaned in closer, needing him every bit as much as he needed her. The kiss they'd shared that afternoon had haunted her for hours. The taste of him, the feel of him, the roaring need pulsing inside her. She'd never known anything like this and she didn't care if he wasn't going to stay. Well, she cared. And wished he would change his mind. But a part of her knew that wouldn't happen. And still she had to have him.

There had been so few perfect moments in her life that she'd learned early to treasure them when they *did* show themselves. And every moment with Sam was perfect. She wanted—*needed*—to feel him inside her again. To feel his strength covering her, opening her, filling her.

And when he was gone—when he left—she would still have these moments to relive. To remember.

His hands, broad-palmed and long-fingered, stroked her spine, then slipped beneath the waistband of her shorts to cup her behind. She sucked in air, then held it as sparklers fired off in her bloodstream. She closed her eyes and concentrated on the sensations he caused. The feel of his hands on her skin—the cold sting of his belt buckle against her belly, the hard ridge of him pressed against her abdomen. Even through the thick fabric of his jeans she felt his heat, his desire, and it fired her blood until she felt as though she were burning up from the inside.

Lifting his head, he stared down into her eyes and whispered a raw confession. "I want you even more than I did the first time."

"I feel exactly the same way," Maggie admitted

and went up on her toes, despite her wobbly knees, to kiss him. Instantly he deepened that kiss, claiming her, devouring her.

He walked her backward until her knees hit the edge of the mattress. Then he laid her down on the bed and came down with her. His hands were everywhere at once. Maggie's eyes closed as she concentrated on the feel of him exploring her every line and curve. Expertly he peeled off her shorts in a matter of seconds and tossed them to the floor. Then he stood up, toed off his boots and yanked his jeans down and off to lie in a sodden heap on the old wooden floorboards.

Then he stopped.

"What?" she demanded impatiently, her body tingling, ready, eager.

"Condom. Still don't have a damn condom."

"In the drawer." She waved a hand at the bedside table and rocked her hips. "I bought some."

He grinned and yanked at the drawer knob. Grabbing up a silver foil packet, he ripped it open, sheathed himself, then came to her, still smiling. "I do like a woman who plans ahead."

His body covered hers and she lifted her hips into him, chewing at her bottom lip. "Enough talking, cowboy. Show me."

"My pleasure," he said and pushed himself into her depths.

Maggie groaned, lifted her legs to wrap them around his hips and drew him deeper, closer. He groaned, too, closing his eyes as the sweet rush of sensation poured through them, connecting them, binding them together in a surge of heat.

He dipped his head to taste her nipples, drawing and suckling her as she rocked beneath him, pulling him close and moaning as his body briefly left hers only to fill her again.

Their bodies linked. They stared into each other's eyes, and when the first shattering explosion came hurtling down on them, they held on to each other and jumped into the abyss.

Ten

Over the next week life at the Lonergan ranch eased into a routine. Days were spent exploring the ranch Sam had known so long ago and nights were spent in Maggie's arms. He'd stopped worrying about what would happen when he left—Maggie was determined to enjoy what they had while they had it, and some of that feeling had seeped into Sam.

And now that Jeremiah's pretense was over, he and Sam spent hours exploring the ranch land together. Years had passed, but the land remained the same—with a few minor changes.

"Vegetables?" Sam asked as he parked the ranch

truck and stared out at long rows of green stretching out as far as the eye could see.

Jeremiah shrugged and squinted into the afternoon sunlight. "Cut way back on running cattle, didn't want the land laying fallow. So I rent this half of the ranch to a group of farmers for a percentage of the net profits. Dave Hemmings rents the grazing land for his dairy herd." He sighed a little and Sam turned to look at him. "I'm an old man, boy. Too much ranch to run alone."

Guilt pinged inside Sam and he tried to ignore the sour stab of it. None of the old man's sons had been interested in the ranch, instead going off to find their own paths. And his grandsons—Sam included—had made themselves scarce fifteen years ago.

Not surprising that Jeremiah would have to make adjustments in how he ran the Lonergan ranch. Still, it stung to realize how much he regretted the necessity. His gaze swept over the neatly tended fields, but in his mind he saw the ranch as it had been years ago—herds of Black Angus cattle wandering over the knee-deep grass.

But times change.

"I'm sorry," he said, still staring out at the neatly tended field of leaf lettuce. "Sorry I wasn't here to help."

Jeremiah reached over and patted Sam's shoulder. His voice gruff, he said, "Never expected you to take on the ranch, boy. It was always doctoring for you.

Will say, though, that I've missed you something terrible. Missed all of you."

"I know." He turned his head to stare at the old man who'd always been so important to him. "And I wish it could have been different. God, Jeremiah, you have no idea how many times I've wished things were different."

"It wasn't your fault, Sam," he said, tiredly. "Wasn't any of you boys' fault."

"Wish I could believe that." He took a breath, blew it out and added, "I missed you, too, you old goat."

Jeremiah's lips twitched and his bushy gray eyebrows wiggled like live caterpillars. "Well, good. Glad to hear it."

"Glad enough to tell me what's going on?" Sam asked. "Why you picked *this* summer to get us all back here?"

"Nope." He shook his head firmly. "Time enough for that once Jake and Cooper show up. Now how about we head into town? Visit Bert?"

Sam narrowed his eyes on his grandfather. "I'm not taking over Bert's practice."

"Who said anything about you?" Jeremiah demanded. "I'm talking about going to see an old friend."

"Uh-huh." Sam wasn't buying it, but he couldn't think of a reason to *not* go. So he put the truck in gear and headed off down the dirt road.

* * *

Maggie lined up all three plastic sticks on the edge of the bathroom sink and swallowed back the knot that was lodged firmly in her throat.

"Three tries," she murmured, shaking her head and staring down at the test results. "Three pluses."

She'd had to be sure. This kind of thing couldn't be trusted to just a "feeling." Though that feeling had been pretty strong. Pretty sure. She was *never* late. If there was one thing in her life that she had always been able to consistently count on, it was the fact that her cycle was as regular as clockwork.

Until this month.

She lifted her head and met her own reflected gaze in the mirror. She deliberately chose to not notice the flicker of worry in her eyes—instead she focused on the joy. All her life she'd longed for family. For someone to love. To love her.

Here at Jeremiah's ranch, she'd found her place.

And now she'd found her family.

"I'm pregnant."

Just saying the words made it all real and brought a tender smile to her face.

Laying both hands protectively against her flat abdomen, she whispered, "Don't worry about a thing, okay, little guy? You'll be okay. I promise."

Even as she said it, though, she felt a flicker of unease as she thought about telling Sam her news. He wouldn't be happy, she knew that already. He was so determined to keep his heart locked away, he would see this baby as an invitation to pain.

Turning around, she sighed and leaned back against the edge of the sink. Her brain raced with thoughts and wishes and half-baked dreams she knew didn't have a chance at becoming reality.

Maggie stared absently at the framed picture of dolphins romping in the sea with children and silently admitted a secret she'd been hiding not only from Sam—but from herself.

She loved him.

She loved Sam Lonergan.

His strength, his tenderness, his gentle touch, even his crabby streak.

She loved everything about him and knew she couldn't keep him. But at least when he left she'd have his child.

And she'd never be alone again.

The waiting room was full.

Babies wailed, harried mothers tried to cope and a tired nurse shouted out the name of the next patient, trying to be heard over the din.

And Sam's instincts were to jump in and help.

Jeremiah strode across the room toward the door leading back to Bert's office, but instead of following him, Sam stopped beside a toddler whimpering softly.

Going down on one knee, he smiled briefly at the boy's mother, then concentrated on the child watching him through wide, anxious, tear-filled eyes.

"What's your name?" Sam asked gently.

"Toby an' my 'froat hurts."

His mother smiled again and said, "He's had a fever since yesterday and I just thought it would be best to bring him in...." She glanced around the crowded waiting room and sighed.

Sam saw the fever shining in the boy's eyes but laid the heel of his palm against the child's forehead anyway. Warm but not bad. Gently he pressed his fingertips against the child's swollen glands and then ruffled light brown featherweight hair. Looking up at the boy's mother, he said, "Looks like tonsillitis. He should be fine with some children's-strength pain reliever. Just make sure he has plenty of fluids."

The woman smiled, then cocked her head to one side and asked, "I'm sorry, but you are...?"

Sam chuckled and straightened up. Not hard to figure out why she was surprised at his spur-of-the-moment diagnosis, dressed as he was in worn jeans, shabby boots and an open-throated, short-sleeved shirt. "Sam Lonergan. Don't worry. I'm an actual doctor."

"Is my 'froat all better now?" The boy's voice was shrill.

"Not yet," Sam said, "but soon." Then he

glanced at the boy's mother. "I'll tell Doc Evans you're out here and—"

She smiled, her eyes brightening even as she stood up and held out one hand. "Thank you. I'm Sally Hoover. This is my son Toby."

Sam smiled. "We've met."

"This is great," she was saying, glancing around the room as if making sure that everyone else there was listening. "You're Jeremiah's grandson, aren't you?"

"Yes…"

"I can't tell you how relieved we all are," Sally continued, rolling right over him as he tried to get in another word or two. "With Doc Evans retiring, most of us thought that we'd have to drive into Fresno to find a new doctor. Having you here is going to make everyone so happy."

Sam backed up. "No, I'm sorry, you don't understand—"

"You're the new doctor?" Another woman, holding an infant tight to her chest, stepped forward, grinning. "I'm Victoria Sanchez, and it's so nice to meet you."

"Thanks, but—"

"I'm Donna Terrino," another woman said from behind him, and Sam spun around to face her. She had twin boys of about five clinging to her legs. It was a wonder she could walk. "This is great. It's a pleasure to have you here," she said. "I can't tell you what this is going to mean to the town."

Panic clawed at Sam's throat.

As more and more of the patients in the waiting room came forward to meet him, faces blurred and names became nothing more than a buzz of conversation around him. His brain raced, his heart pounded.

He felt…trapped.

They were all looking at him as though he were a longed-for Christmas present. They wouldn't let him speak long enough to shatter their illusions, and damned if a part of him wasn't grateful. He didn't want to be here to see the disappointment on their faces. Didn't want to care that he'd be leaving the town he'd once loved in the lurch.

It wasn't his responsibility.

The welfare of the town's health care wasn't up to him.

So why then did the guilt crawling through him feel so much bigger? Stronger?

"When will you be setting up your own practice?" someone in the back of the crowd asked.

"Is he the new doctor?" a child called out.

No, he wanted to shout but doubted any of them would pay attention. They already had him hanging out his shingle and seeing his first patient. A yearning he hadn't quite expected darted through him, then was gone again in the next heartbeat. Just as well. It didn't matter if a part of him wished he *could* settle here, be the man they all wanted him to be.

The door into the hallway opened up behind him and Sam turned to try to make a break for it. He took one step though and stopped dead.

"Sam?" The big man coming through the door tightened his grip on the little girl at his side and marched toward Sam with long, measured strides.

Memories kicked in and Sam momentarily forgot about looking for the fastest way out. "Mike? Mike Haney?"

"Damn straight," the big man said, grinning. "Good to see you, man," he added. "It's been way too long. I heard you were back in town. Cooper and Jake here, too?"

"Not yet," Sam said, ignoring the chattering mothers and crying babies surrounding them. Mike Haney had been a good friend years ago. He was only one of the people in Coleville that Sam had missed. "Soon, though."

"This is my daughter," Mike was saying, tugging a blond girl out from behind him.

"Your *daughter?*" Hard to believe. In Sam's mind, Mike Haney and all of his other friends were still seventeen years old. Still swiping beers from their fathers' refrigerators to meet out at the lake and lie to each other about their conquests.

Proudly Mike said, "We—me and Barb—you remember Barb?"

"Sure," Sam said, still bemused by the blond-haired cutie half hiding behind her father. Then it clicked. "You and Barb got married?"

"Sure did—and this little beauty is our youngest. I've got three girls now."

"Three…"

"And every one of 'em's a heartbreaker. How about you?" Mike asked, smiling. "Wife and kids?"

"No," Sam said and suddenly felt the punch of all that he'd missed by avoiding any relationship that looked like it might grow into something important. "No family."

"Oh, well…" Mike hemmed and hawed for a moment or two, then tugged his daughter out to say hello. "Want you to meet Maxie—" He paused and added, "We named her after Mac. Maxie, honey, say hi to Dr. Sam. He's an old friend of your daddy's."

Sam stared into wide blue eyes and tried to find a smile. But the sudden thickening in his throat made it damn near impossible. Mac. The reason he'd stayed away so long. The reason he had to leave again. Soon.

"She's beautiful," Sam finally managed to say, then edged past his old friend, heading for the relative sanctuary of Bert's office. The waiting room was still filled with excited chatter. The little blond girl gave him a finger wave. "It was good to see you again, Mike."

The big man nodded, oblivious to Sam's eager

escape. "You let me know when Jake and Cooper hit town. We'll get together. Talk about old times."

"Right. Good idea." *Never gonna happen*, he thought. No way did he want to sit down and reminisce.

And he was pretty sure both Jake and Cooper would feel the same way.

Maggie waited.

All through dinner, through doing the dishes, cleaning the kitchen and even through the evening news. She held her secret close and waited until Jeremiah had fallen asleep in front of the television and she and Sam were alone.

And now that they were, she wasn't at all sure how to say what had to be said.

He sat at the kitchen table, the ranch accounting books laid out in front of him. Turning from the sink, she stared at him for a long minute and let the knots in her stomach slowly tighten.

His dark hair fell across his forehead as he bent his head to look at a row of figures. He trailed his long fingers down the line of numbers slowly as he checked and rechecked the totals at the bottom. Leaning to one side, he flipped through a stack of papers and sifted through them until he found the one he was looking for.

The quiet drone of the television played in the background, and outside, the wind tapped against the windows with chilly fingers.

Maggie sighed, dried her hands on the dish towel, then carefully hooked it over the handle on the oven door to dry. This wasn't going to get any easier. Best, she thought, to just say it and say it fast.

"Sam?"

"Hmm?" He didn't even look up. Just scribbled a notation on a legal-size yellow pad of paper to his right.

"I need to talk to you."

"Sure," he said, making another note.

"It's important."

The hesitant tone of her voice must have gotten through to him because he set his pencil down and swiveled his head to look at her. Frowning slightly, he asked, "Something wrong?"

"No," she said, though she was forced to admit that *he* might see things a little differently. What was to her a gift, Sam would no doubt consider a trap. A trap she had no intention of springing on him. "At least," she amended slightly, "*I* don't consider it a problem."

He gave her a brief smile. "Now I'm intrigued." Standing up, he crossed the room to her. Glancing into the living room to make sure Jeremiah was still sleeping in his recliner, he looked back at Maggie. "What's going on?"

She drew a deep breath, blew it out in a long rush and then tried a smile of her own. "I've been practicing all day just how to tell you this and now that I'm here—"

He cupped her face in his palms. "Just say it, Maggie."

"Right." She lifted her hands to cover his. A flutter of warmth filled Maggie as she looked up into his dark eyes. Joy and misery twisted inside her as she realized that if things had been different, this moment might have been a celebration.

She wanted to tell him how much she loved him. How much she would *always* love him. But she knew that confession wouldn't be any more welcome than the one she was about to make.

The truth was undeniable, though. She loved a man who had no intention of loving her in return. A man whose only thought was to leave as quickly as he could. Her heart ached at the knowledge of all they might have had together, all they would never share.

"You're starting to worry me, Maggie," he said, his voice a low hush of sound barely discernable over the rumble of the TV.

"Don't," she said, shaking her head. "Don't worry about me. I'm fine. Better than fine."

It didn't matter, she realized suddenly. Didn't matter if he would never love her. It was enough that *she* loved.

"Let's go outside," she said, stepping away from him and heading for the back door. She didn't want to tell him here—with Jeremiah snoring in the other room.

He followed her, and once outside, Maggie kept

walking until she was standing in the middle of the yard, with the pale wash of moonlight covering her. He stopped alongside her and said, "Okay, we're outside. Now tell me."

"I'm going to," she said and swallowed hard. "But before I do, I want you to know I don't expect anything from you. I'm only telling you because it's the right thing to do."

"Maggie…"

"I'm pregnant."

Eleven

Sam felt like he'd been hit over the head.

Pregnant?

He scraped one hand across his face and tried to think of something—hell, *anything*—to say. But it was impossible with the flurry of thoughts racing through his mind. A *baby*. It felt as though a cold fist was squeezing his heart, and damned if that thought didn't make him ashamed.

He'd made a child with Maggie. Whether he'd meant to or not, the deed was done.

"You don't have to say anything," Maggie told him quickly.

He blew out a breath as his gaze fixed on her.

Moonlight draped over her like a pale cloak, and her eyes shone with it—that and a joy he hadn't noticed before. Clearly she was pleased about this pregnancy.

He wished he could be.

Instead fear grabbed the base of his throat and held on tight. Not something he wanted to admit to. Not even to himself. But it was there.

"How long have you known?" he finally managed to ask.

"Since this morning," she said, reaching out to lay one hand on his forearm. "Sam, I know this isn't something you wanted, but I'm *glad* about it. Believe me."

"I can see that." Her smile wasn't forced, but there was concern now flickering in her eyes. Concern for *him.*

"I don't expect anything from you, Sam," she said and lifted her chin proudly. "I only told you because it was the right thing to do. You have a right to know that you're going to be a father."

"God. A father." A part of him hungered for it. For the rush of expectation. For the simple pleasure of having a child. A home. And a woman like Maggie to love.

"You don't have to look so spooked," she said, forcing a smile that didn't reach her eyes. "It's not like I'm about to go into labor or anything."

"I know, it's just—"

The wind whipped past them, lifting her hair into a tangle of dark strands around her head. She pushed them out of her face and kept her gaze locked with his. "I want you to know you don't have to worry about me—or the baby. I'll take good care of him—her—it."

"I know that." He nodded while thoughts and plans ran wildly through his mind. Maggie was smart, capable, funny. She could handle anything. She'd proved that just by living her life. As a kid, she'd been given a hard road. But she'd made herself the life she'd always wanted. He had no doubt at all that she could care for their child just as well.

But she shouldn't have to.

Every instinct he possessed was telling him what to do. What to say next. "I can't let you do this alone, Maggie. This baby is my responsibility, too."

Her eyes narrowed. "Meaning…?"

"Meaning," he said, straightening his spine and accepting his duty even as he inwardly worried about it, "I want you to marry me."

She staggered back a step from him, looking at him as though he'd grown another head. Safe to say he'd surprised her. Well, he'd surprised the hell out of himself, too.

"What?"

"You heard me. We should get married. Like you said before, it's the right thing to do." It was easier to say the second time. What did that mean? He didn't have time to search for answers. "It's my child, too, Maggie. It deserves to have its father."

The surprise etched on her features faded into sorrow as she shook her head slowly. "Oh, Sam. If I thought that was what you really wanted, I'd be so happy."

"It *is*," he said and wondered briefly if he was trying to convince her or himself.

"No," she said and unshed tears glimmered in her eyes. When she spoke again, her voice broke, but she lifted her chin as if trying to gather the strength she needed. "It's not. You don't want roots. You don't want love. You don't want me—or this baby."

"Maggie—"

"Don't, Sam," she said and took a step toward him. "Don't say something you don't really mean."

In the soft light of the moon he read regret and disappointment and *understanding* in her eyes. It almost killed him.

"We both know," she continued gently, "that if you stayed, you'd never be happy. Eventually you'd resent me and even the baby for trying to hold you."

Hard to argue with the simple truth, but God, he wanted to. Wanted to be a different man. Wanted to *feel* differently. But how could he?

"I want to say you're wrong," he said, "but I just don't know. For fifteen years," he whispered, choking the words out through a strangled throat, "I've been running from the demons chasing me. I loved Mac and I failed him and he *died*. That's something I can't change. And if I loved you and our baby and failed you the same way, I don't think I could stand it."

A small, sad smile curved her mouth as she reached up and cupped his cheek in her palm. "And that's why I can't marry you, Sam. Even though I love you."

He felt the punch of those words as he would have a fist to the midsection. Everything in him wanted to grab her, pull her close and hang on. To savor the words he'd never thought to hear. Never thought to *want* to hear. But the look on her face warned him to keep still.

"Yes, I love you. But I can't marry you, Sam, because I want our baby to be raised with love, not fear. To feel faith, not despair."

He covered her hand with one of his own and held on as if the touch meant his life. "I wish it could be different." And even while he said it, he knew the words were useless. Knew that saying it, *wanting* it, didn't make it so.

"That's the sad part," Maggie said, slipping her hand from his. "It *could* be different. You just won't let it be."

"It's not that simple."

"Yes, it is," she said. "You say you've been running from the demons chasing you—but that's not true, either."

"What?"

"It's not demons chasing you, Sam," she said, her voice soft and filled with pain. "It's only *Mac*. And he loves you."

His features tightened and Maggie *felt* him emotionally withdraw. She wanted to cry but knew it wouldn't help. She wanted to *reach* him and knew that though he was standing right in front of her, he was further away from her than ever.

And just like that, a piece of her heart died. Swallowing back the tears gathering in her throat, she said only, "I don't want a husband who thinks it's his *duty* to marry me."

"Maggie…"

"I think it's best if you leave at the end of summer, just as you planned. I don't want you to be a part of the baby's life."

He swayed as if she'd physically struck him. "It's my baby, too, Maggie."

"Yes, but you don't want him. *I* do."

"Damn it, Maggie—"

Whatever else he might have said was forgotten as a sweep of headlights sliced across the darkened yard, flashing briefly in Maggie's eyes. She turned her head and squinted at the SUV pulling into the yard and parking just a few feet from them.

The lights blinked into darkness and the engine was cut off. The driver's-side door opened and a tall man with broad shoulders and hair as dark as Sam's stepped out and walked toward them.

"Looks like I'm interrupting something," the man said, glancing from Maggie to Sam and back again. "My timing always sucked."

"Cooper," Sam said, walking toward him and holding out one hand. They shook hands, then Sam turned and said, "Cooper, this is Maggie Collins. She's...Jeremiah's housekeeper."

She winced inwardly at the distance in Sam's voice but told herself it was just as well that Cooper had arrived to stop their conversation. They only would have ended up going around and around in a never-ending cycle of pain.

"Nice to meet you," she managed to say, then tore her gaze from Cooper Lonergan to focus on Sam again. "I'll see you in the morning."

"Maggie..."

She backed up a step or two, said, "G'night, Sam. Cooper." Then she turned and hurried across the moonlit yard to her own house. Stepping inside, she closed the door behind her and leaned back against it.

Knees weak, heart breaking, she closed her eyes and gave herself up to the pain.

"So you want to tell me what's going on here?" Cooper asked after Jeremiah had gone off to bed. "I still can't believe he tricked all of us."

"Yeah, surprised the hell out of me, too." Sam took a couple of beers from the refrigerator, handed one to his cousin and motioned him down into a chair. Twisting off the cap, he took a long pull of the icy beverage, relishing the taste of the cold froth. Swallowing, he took a seat himself and explained everything he knew about Jeremiah and his pretense of dying.

When he was finished, Cooper laughed shortly and took a drink of his beer. "I'll give him this…I'm so glad he's *not* dying, I'm not even mad at him."

"Same goes."

"Who would have guessed that the old man could be that sneaky? Hell, that creative?"

Smiling wryly, Sam acknowledged, "Must run in the family." Cooper Lonergan's horror novels had been giving Americans nightmares for the last five years. Each of his books was just a little creepier than the last. And the fact that Cooper was pretty much a recluse only added to his appeal.

Leaning back in his seat, Sam cradled his beer bottle between his palms and said, "I read your latest book."

"Yeah?" Cooper asked. "What'd you think?"

"Spooky," he admitted. "Just like all the others."

A tired smile crossed Cooper's face briefly. "Thanks." He looked around the familiar room and sighed a little. "Man, nothing here has changed at all. Like stepping into a time warp or something."

"Saw Mike Haney in town," Sam offered.

"No kidding?" Cooper chuckled, remembering. "How is he?"

"Married to Barb Hawkins with three little girls."

"Man," Cooper said after another long drink. "We're old."

Sam stared across the table at the cousin he hadn't seen since they were kids. Except for getting taller and broader in the shoulders, Cooper looked pretty much the same as he had all those years ago. And in his dark Lonergan eyes Sam recognized the same shadows he faced every morning when he looked in a mirror.

Mac's death had affected them all.

"So want to tell me about the housekeeper?"

Sam stiffened, took a drink of beer and asked, "Tell you what?"

Cooper chuckled. "Don't get so defensive. It just looked like you two were talking about something…*important*."

Setting his beer on the table, Sam stood up, walked across the kitchen to the pantry and yanked the door open. Grabbing up a plastic container filled with cookies, he opened it and walked back to the table. He took a couple for himself, then shoved the tub toward Cooper.

"What kind?"

"Chocolate chip."

"With *beer?*" Cooper asked.

"Something wrong with that?" Sam demanded,

taking a bite and then washing it down with another drink of beer.

"Not a thing." Taking a bite, Cooper chewed and stared at the cookie as if it were made of gold. "These are amazing."

"Yeah." Sam grumbled the word and thought about how good Maggie had looked yesterday while she'd been baking these cookies. She'd had flour on her nose and her hair in a crooked ponytail and she'd danced a quick two-step in time with country music streaming from the radio. He'd had a hell of a time refraining from throwing her onto the floor and burying himself inside her.

Every move she made touched him like nothing else ever had. Every one of her smiles lit up his insides. Her touch was silk. Her taste intoxicating.

He wanted her with every breath.

"Hell," Cooper said, leaning forward to grab a handful of cookies from the tub, "is she married?"

"Why?" One word. Snarled.

"Whoa," Cooper said, holding up both cookie-filled hands in mock surrender. "Don't shoot. I was just asking."

Sam blew out a breath. "Sorry."

"So she's spoken for, then?"

"Leave it alone, will ya, Cooper?"

"Right." A couple of long minutes passed before he spoke again, and when he did, it was to offer a change of subject—for which Sam was grateful. "If Jeremiah's not dying, why *are* we here?"

"He won't say," Sam told him. "Not until we're all here. Have you heard anything from Jake?"

"I talked to him right after we got the news about Jeremiah. Said he'd get here as soon as he could. But he had some things to wrap up where he was first."

"Spain?"

Cooper shrugged. "You know Jake. He'll go anywhere for a race."

The night crouched outside the brightly lit kitchen and the wind began to whisper at the windowpanes. The old house was quiet but for the few creaks and groans it made as it settled, like an ancient woman lowering herself into a chair.

"It *is* good to see you," Sam said.

"You, too. We never should have let it go so long. I've missed you guys."

"Me, too." Sam picked at the damp label on the beer bottle. His cousins had once been the best part of his life. Losing all of them had cost him more than he wanted to think about.

Silence stretched out until all they heard was the ticking of the clock, like a heartbeat, measuring time. Then finally setting his unfinished beer on the table, Connor stood up and said, "I'd better get going."

"You sure you don't want to stay here?"

"I'm sure. I mean, I'm glad to see you. And

Jeremiah. But the memories are a little thick in this old house."

Sam couldn't argue with that one.

"Besides," he said, picking up his long black coat off the back of a kitchen chair, "I've got to work while I'm here, and with all of us staying here, that'll never happen."

Sam nodded and followed his cousin as he walked out of the kitchen. "Can't believe you rented the Hollis place," he said. "People still say it's haunted."

Cooper stopped, one hand on the car door, and grinned at his cousin. "Why the hell do you think I picked that place? What better house for a horror writer to live in for the summer?"

"Right."

"I'll see you tomorrow."

Sam nodded and lifted one hand as Cooper steered his rental car out of the yard and headed for the main road.

When the grumble of the car's engine had died away and the only sound was that of leaves being pushed along the dirt by the wind, Sam turned to look at Maggie's house. One light was burning—in her bedroom.

He wanted to go to her. Hold her and feel her warmth wrap itself around him. But he doubted she felt like seeing him at the moment. Sam shoved his hands into his back pockets and kept his gaze fixed on that slice of golden light framed in her bedroom window.

He pictured her there, in her bed, under the flowered quilt, and he wondered what she was thinking. Feeling.

Did she feel as empty as he did?

Was she lonely?

Or was the child growing within her enough to keep the shadows at bay?

Twelve

Over the next few days Jeremiah seemed to get ten years younger. His smile was broader, his eyes brighter and his laugh just a little louder.

Sam watched the older man and felt the sharp teeth of guilt take another bite out of him. He'd stayed away for his own selfish reasons but had never considered that he was punishing his family, too.

He hadn't only avoided the Lonergan ranch and his grandfather, he'd also managed to ignore his parents in his own need to keep moving. To keep running from the shadows chasing him.

And now it was too late to make it up to them. Both of his parents had died five years ago in a small-plane crash. The old man's other three sons were also gone now. Accidents, mostly. As if the Lonergan family were cursed. The only family he had left now were his cousins and grandfather.

He was only just realizing how important they were to him. How important *living* was to him.

All because of Maggie.

Shaking his head, he pulled the worn brown leather work gloves off his hands, tucked them in the waistband of his jeans, then pulled off his T-shirt. The morning sun was already heating up, and sweat streamed down his chest and back.

It felt good.

Good to be standing still rather than running.

Good to be working on a place that still held such a large part of his heart.

His gaze swept the yard and the surrounding fields as he tossed his damp shirt across the closest fence post. In the last few weeks this place had gotten to him again, as it had when he was a kid. And the thought of leaving was more painful than he'd expected.

But that probably had more to do with *who* he'd be leaving this time. Slowly he shifted his gaze to the small house where Maggie lived. She wasn't home. He knew that. And yet…something of her remained even when she was gone.

For a few weeks he'd found peace in her arms.

He'd found solace and comfort and a sense of *home-coming* that he'd never known before. Yet even while he enjoyed those feelings, they terrified him. Because he couldn't stay. Couldn't be what she wanted—*needed*.

Could he?

"How can one man have so many questions and so few answers?" he muttered, pushing his hair back from his face and tipping his head back. He stared up at the brilliant blue sky shimmering with the heat of the sun. He felt the sunlight on his face, the heat slipping into him as his skin baked.

And still he felt cold.

Right down to his bones.

The worst of it was he had the distinct feeling that it was all his own damn fault.

A car's engine grumbled into the silence, and Sam turned, hoping that Jeremiah and Cooper were back from the homecoming tour of Coleville the old man had insisted on. God knew, Sam was tired of his own company. Too much time to think gave a man way too much room for self-reflection.

But it wasn't Cooper's rented SUV roaring into the yard. It was the ranch truck, with Maggie at the wheel.

Instantly Sam's heartbeat quickened and his mouth went dry. Sunlight glanced off the windshield, throwing a wide enough glare that he couldn't see her. Strangely enough, though, that didn't seem to matter. Just knowing she was close had his body tightening and his long-suppressed emotions racing.

She opened the truck door and climbed down, tossing her hair back over her shoulder as she glanced at him. "Hello, Sam."

Her smile was soft and sad and tugged at the corners of his heart. God, he missed her. Missed being with her. Missed laughing with her, talking with her.

And when he left her, he didn't know how he'd make it without her.

"Is Jeremiah back yet?" she asked, closing the door and reaching over the side of the truck for the sacks of groceries in the flatbed.

"No," Sam said ,already heading for her.

"I thought I'd make a chocolate cake—a *celebration* since the two of you are here." She went up on her toes, grabbed two plastic sacks and started to lift them.

"Don't," Sam said, stepping up to brush her hands away and grab the bags himself. Shooting her a quick warning look, he said, "You shouldn't be lifting heavy things. Not now."

She smiled up at him. "I'm fine, Sam. The baby's fine. And I can carry groceries myself."

Stung, he paid no attention and gathered up the bags anyway, lifting them over the edge of the truck's side before looking at her again. "You're not going to. Not while I'm here."

Something flickered in her eyes and her smile faded. "I'll have to do it when you leave."

A cold fist tightened around his heart and gave it a squeeze that sent pain shooting through him. "I'm not gone yet," he reminded her.

"Okay, then. Just set them on the kitchen counter." She waved a hand at the main house and then led the way. She opened the back door and held it so he could go in first, and as he set the bags down, she started unloading them.

"I can do that, too," he said, suddenly needing to help. To do what he could, *while* he could.

She set a box of cake mix onto the counter and looked up at him. "Sam, I know you're only trying to be nice, but—"

"Maggie, it's important to me to...*help.*" Damn, that sounded pretty lame, even to him. Help? He was going to help the mother of his child unload groceries now and then leave her completely in another couple of months? Yeah. Great plan.

She sighed and reached up to him, touching him for the first time in days. Her fingertips against his cheek felt cool and soft and more wonderful than anything else he'd ever experienced. God, he'd missed her touch.

And just when he was giving himself up to the sweet rush of sensation, she let her hand drop again. He tried not to notice just how empty he felt.

"Sam, I can't do this," she said softly, her eyes glimmering with a sheen of tears she determinedly refused to allow to fall. "I can't…be *close* to you and not love you."

"Maggie—"

She lifted one hand to quiet him. "And I can't love you and think about you leaving. I'm sorry. I really am. But if you want to help me, then please… just give me some space."

A flush of remorse and shame swept through him and Sam took a step back from her, though that one small action cost him. It felt as though dozens of knives were slicing off tiny sections of his heart, whittling it down to a cold, hard stone that would be with him for the rest of his life.

But this wasn't about him. "You're right. I'll, uh, go back out and finish fixing the fence." He turned for the back door and stopped, one hand on the knob. "Just…do me a favor and don't lift anything heavy."

She forced a smile that looked as empty as he felt. "I won't."

"Thanks. I'll be out—" He broke off when the phone rang and Maggie stepped to one side to snatch the receiver off the wall hook.

"Lonergan ranch," she said, fingering the old phone's twisted yellow cord. "Hi, Susan. What's—oh. Okay, I'll tell him. Yes," she said, glancing at Sam, "he's right here. Okay, tell Katie not to worry."

When she hung up, Sam asked, "What's wrong?"

"That was Susan Bateman. Their dog's in labor and little Katie's terrified that something 'bad' will happen. She wants *you* to come and help."

"Me?" Sam laughed shortly and then frowned. "Katie knows I'm a people doctor, right?"

"Yes," Maggie said, "but she's a little girl who loves her dog. She's scared. And she trusts you."

Trust.

A heavy burden.

Especially to a man who kept trying to step back from people and all of their expectations.

Maggie sensed his withdrawal and wanted to cry. But then, since finding out she was pregnant, she'd done a lot of crying. It shouldn't be this hard, she thought. Being in love, having a child…she should be *happy*. Celebrating the wonder of it all.

Instead she was already in mourning for the loss of the man who couldn't—or *wouldn't*—see what was right in front of him.

"You said you wanted to help me," she said softly, watching his eyes, seeing the wariness and sighing for it. "If you really mean that, then go help Katie."

His jaw worked as if he were chewing on words that tasted bitter. Finally, though, he nodded. "All right. I'll be back later."

Then he was gone, and Maggie leaned against

the kitchen counter wishing she could change things. Wishing he could see that they belonged together. The three of them.

The dog wasn't interested in his help.

A pale yellow golden retriever, she gave Sam a look that clearly said, *If you'll just keep out of my way, I'll be done in a bit.*

So he did. Sitting with Katie, Sam watched as the fifth puppy pushed itself into the world, then wriggled blindly until it found its way to its mother's side.

"Does it hurt?" Katie asked, keeping a viselike grip on his index finger.

"A little," he said, but added quickly, pointing at the dog lying on a bed of blankets, "but Duchess doesn't seem to mind, does she?"

"No." Katie scooted around to sit on Sam's lap. "Look, another one!"

Sure enough, a sixth puppy was born, and after a few minutes numbers seven and eight made their appearance. Soon all of the puppies were cleaned up to their mother's satisfaction and happily nursing while Duchess took a well-deserved nap.

"Mommy, they're all here," Katie called out.

Susan Bateman poked her head into the service-porch area and gave Sam a smile. "Thanks for coming over. She was so worried."

"It's not a problem," he said.

"You can have a puppy if you want," Katie said, tipping her head back so she could look at him. "Jeremiah wants one, and you could have one, too."

"Oh, honey," Susan said quickly, giving Sam an apologetic smile. "Dr. Sam's not going to be staying here. And he doesn't really have a home, so he couldn't have a dog with him."

He frowned a little, not much liking the explanation, but what could he say? She was right.

"You don't have a house?"

"No," he started to say.

"He's a busy man," Susan said for him. "He works all over the world."

"But you don't hafta," Katie said, leaning back into him and giving his hand a pat. "You could stay 'n' have a dog 'n' a house 'n' a little girl for me to play wif 'n'—"

"Katie..." Her mother sounded tired but amused. "Why don't you go upstairs, wash your hands for lunch."

"Oooookaaaaaayyy..." Clearly disgusted, Katie did as she was told.

Once she was gone, Susan shrugged and said, "Thanks for coming over. It meant a lot to Katie."

"No problem," he said, standing up and brushing his palms together. "Happy to help."

She didn't look as if she believed him, but she

smiled anyway. "Some people think I spoil Katie, I know, but it's hard not to."

"She's an only child?"

"Actually, no," she said softly. "We had two children. But our son, Jacob, died two years ago."

Her quiet voice, the simple words, shook him hard.

"I don't know what to say," he said helplessly.

"It's okay. No reason why you should. Come with me, I want to show you something." She gave him a smile and led the way into the living room. Sunlight slashed through a wide bay window to lay across over-stuffed furniture and a faded braided rug on the gleaming wood floor. It was a big room, cozily crowded with kids' toys, magazines spread across a wide coffee table and several books stacked on an end table.

Susan walked to the far wall, where dozens of framed snapshots and collages of family pictures cluttered the wall with smiling faces. There, she showed him a studio portrait of a laughing boy about three years old with pale blond hair and shining blue eyes just like his sister's. "That's Jacob."

"He's beautiful." Sam slanted her a look and felt his heart break a little to know that child had died. Looking back at the child who would forever be three years old. "What happened?"

She sighed, folded her arms across her chest and said simply, "When we moved in here, we'd planned to put in a fence out front. But we hadn't gotten around to it yet." Her voice went faint, distant. "We got *busy*." She shook herself and added, "Jacob chased a ball into the street. The driver of the car never saw him."

God. "I'm so sorry."

"So were we," she said quietly and turned to look at him as she took a long, deep breath to steady herself. "It took a long time, but life finally goes on anyway. We still have our memories of Jacob. And we have Katie and—" she patted her flat abdomen, "number three is on his way."

Even after experiencing something no parent should have to live through, she'd found a way to go on. To try again. Touched by her courage, Sam asked, "How do you get past the pain?"

"You don't," she said. "You just learn to live with it. But you know that already. Jeremiah's told me about your cousin Mac."

Some of us live with it, Sam thought, as Susan left to check on Katie, and some of us run from it. It shamed him to admit that this woman showed more quiet courage every day of her life than he'd been able to find in the last fifteen years.

And in the next instant his world suddenly came into focus. Heart pounding, eyes stinging, throat tight, he finally *got it*. Finally understood that running wasn't healing. That hiding from pain didn't protect you. That unless he found a way to *really* live again, he was just as dead as Mac.

* * *

"I'm sorry, Mac," Sam said, staring out over the dark, still water of the lake. Strange as it seemed, he could have sworn that he *felt* Mac's presence. And he was grateful for it. "Sorry I let you down that day. Sorry it took me so long to come back here."

The wind kicked up and ripples spun across the surface of the lake, spreading out from edge to edge in a silent, inexorable march.

"I still miss you. Every damn day." He bent down, picked up a rock and tossed it high and far, watching it until it splashed down in the center of the water and quickly sank beneath the surface. "But I think I'm finally going to be okay. I just...wanted you to know that."

Then he stood in the silence, and for the first time since that summer day so long ago, he felt...*alive*.

A knock on her door startled Maggie enough that she spilled her hot tea down the front of her pale green shirt. Glancing at the door, she fought down a surge of excitement and told herself to get a grip.

Sam hadn't come to her since the day she'd told him about the baby. And that was the way she wanted it.

Right?

Muttering under her breath, she set her mug down on the coffee table and stood up. She crossed the room, opened the door and stared up at Sam.

But this was a *different* Sam than the man she'd seen a few hours ago. This man's eyes were alive with joy, with hope, and she felt a quick jolt of something like hope herself.

"Sam?"

"Can I come in, Maggie?" Both of his hands were braced on the doorjamb as if he were actually holding himself back from charging into the room.

"I don't know—" Hope was there, but she couldn't let herself believe. Couldn't set herself up for disappointment.

"Please, Maggie. There's so much I want to tell you—*ask* you."

Chills swept up and down her spine and she swallowed hard as she followed her instincts. Stepping back, she waved him inside. He strode in with a few long steps that carried him to the center of the room. Then he turned to look at her.

"Maggie, I'm an idiot."

"Okay…" She closed the door quietly and waited, afraid to believe. Afraid to wish.

He pushed both hands through his hair, then let his hands drop to his sides. "Something clicked for me today."

"What?"

"You. Us. The baby." He laughed and threw his hands wide. "*Life.*"

Frowning, she stepped away from the door and walked a few steps closer to him. "What're you talking about, Sam?"

"I love you."

She staggered and slapped one hand to her chest as if she could hold her foolishly thumping heart in place. "What?"

"I *love* you, Maggie," he repeated and came toward her. "I think I have from the first time I saw you. I was just too stupid—or too *scared*—to realize it. To let myself believe in it."

"Sam, I don't know what to say…." *Oh, God,* she prayed silently, *please let him mean this.*

"Don't say anything. Let me talk. Let me tell you what you mean to me." He came to her, cupped her face between his palms and stared down into her eyes. "You reminded me what it was like to live again, Maggie. You laughed with me, argued with me. You showed me that life without love isn't life at all."

"Sam…" Her voice broke and she blinked away tears that were blinding her. She didn't want to miss this. Didn't want to be blinded to the emotions flashing in his eyes.

"I've spent fifteen years running," he said, his fingers spearing through her hair as his gaze moved over her features slowly, like a lover's touch. "I've hidden away from everything and everyone I loved. I lost time with people who were important to me. Time I can *never* get back. I clung to guilt because I thought I wasn't allowed to be happy. I buried my feelings because to care about someone meant risking that horrific pain again."

She reached up and touched his cheek, felt the scrape of his whiskers against her palm and smiled when he turned his face into her touch and kissed the heart of her hand.

"But, Maggie, today I realized that *not* risking love brings its own kind of pain." He pulled her closer and watched her eyes. "I've been alone and empty. I don't want to be alone anymore, Maggie. I want to love you. I want to *be* loved by you. I want to raise our baby—and all the other babies we'll have together."

"All?" she managed to squeak.

"*All,*" he said with a wild laugh. "Let's have a dozen."

"Sam…"

"I'm ready to risk it all again, Maggie. I'm ready to have faith. To believe. And what I believe in is *you.*"

Everything in her went warm and gooey. She felt as though if he let go of her, she might just ooze into a puddle on the floor. It was more. So much more than she'd hoped for—prayed for. "Oh, Sam, I—"

He talked right over her, his excitement coloring his voice. "I already talked to Doc Evans. I'm going to take over his practice in town—"

"You are?" Eyes wide, she grinned, overwhelmed by him, by the knowledge of the future they were going to share after all.

"But if it's okay with you, I'd like to live *here*. At the ranch. Jeremiah's getting up there and he could use the help, and damn it, I want my family back. I want my roots. This place."

Maggie laughed through her tears. "Of *course* it's okay with me. This is my home. I love it here. I love Jeremiah."

"And me?" he asked breathlessly. "Please tell me you still love me, Maggie. Please tell me I haven't waited too long."

"I love you, Sam," she said, her heart in her voice, her tears blinding her completely. But it didn't matter now. Because she knew she'd be able to see him every day. She'd always be able to see the light of love in his eyes. "I'll *always* love you."

"Then you'll marry me?" he asked and sounded a little nervous about it.

"Yes, I'll marry you," she whispered and felt her heart fill to bursting. "And I swear I will love you forever."

As he pulled her in for a kiss, he whispered, "That may not be long enough, Maggie. Not nearly long enough."

* * * * *

Maureen Child's SUMMER OF SECRETS series continues with STRICTLY LONERGAN'S BUSINESS, *available in May from Silhouette Desire.*

THE
ELLIOTTS

Mixing business with pleasure

continues with

MR. AND MISTRESS
(SD #1723)

HEIDI BETTS

She had been his kept woman...
until she discovered she was
pregnant with his child.
Did she dare reveal her
secret pregnancy?

On Sale May 2006

Available at your favorite retail outlet!

Silhouette®

BOMBSHELL™

ATHENA FORCE

CHOSEN FOR THEIR TALENTS.
TRAINED TO BE THE BEST.
EXPECTED TO CHANGE THE WORLD.

The women of Athena Academy are back.
Don't miss their compelling new adventures
as they reveal the truth about their founder's
unsolved murder—and provoke the wrath of a
cunning new enemy....

FLASHBACK
by Justine DAVIS

Available April 2006 at your favorite retail outlet.

MORE ATHENA ADVENTURES
COMING SOON:

Look-Alike by Meredith Fletcher, May 2006
Exclusive by Katherine Garbera, June 2006
Pawn by Carla Cassidy, July 2006
Comeback by Doranna Durgin, August 2006

**Silhouette Desire
presents the latest
Westmoreland title from**

BRENDA
JACKSON

THE DURANGO AFFAIR

(SD #1727)

Durango Westmoreland's bachelor
days are numbered when an
unforgettable night of passion with
hazel-eyed Savannah Claiborne
results in a big surprise...and
a hasty trip to the altar.

On Sale May 2006

Available at your favorite retail outlet!

COMING NEXT MONTH

#1723 MR. AND MISTRESS—Heidi Betts
The Elliotts
Scandal threatens to rock the Elliott family when a business mogul wants to make his pregnant mistress his wife!

#1724 STRICTLY LONERGAN'S BUSINESS—
Maureen Child
Summer of Secrets
She was his ever-dependent, quiet assistant…until a month of sharing close quarters finally allowed her to catch her boss's eye.

#1725 THE RAGS-TO-RICHES-WIFE—Metsy Hingle
Secrets Lives of Society Wives
After a secret rendezvous leads to an unplanned pregnancy, this Cinderella finds herself a high-society wife of convenience.

#1726 DEVLIN AND THE DEEP BLUE SEA—
Merline Lovelace
Code Name: Danger
He was a mystery to solve and she was just the woman to uncover *all* of his secrets!

#1727 THE DURANGO AFFAIR—Brenda Jackson
Having an affair with a man like Durango was like lighting a match during a drought—fast to ignite, hot to burn, impossible to quench.

#1728 HOUSE OF MIDNIGHT FANTASIES—Kristi Gold
Rich and Reclusive
Reading your boss's mind can lead to trouble…*especially* when you're the one he's fantasizing about.

SDCNM0406